A Liar?

"Listen Norrie," she said turning. "You have to decide. Do you want Mark, or don't you?"

I thought I'd given up on Mark, but now that Steff was asking me point-blank, I knew I'd been lying to myself. "Yes," I admitted. "I want him desperately. More than anything. . . ."

"Look, I'm not saying you should lie to him, but there's no reason to make a big confession scene, either. Just be cool. And for Chrissake, don't tell him the truth. . . ."

Also by Laura Sonnenmark:

Something's Rotten in the State of Maryland

THE LIE

LAURA SONNENMARK

SCHOLASTIC INC.
New York Toronto London Auckland Sydney

No part of this publication may be reproduced in whole or in part, or stored in a retrieval system, or transmitted in any form or by any means, electronic, mechanical, photocopying, recording, or otherwise, without written permission of the publisher. For information regarding permission, write to Scholastic Inc., 555 Broadway, New York, NY 10012.

ISBN 0-590-44741-6

12 11 10 9 8 7 6 5 4 3 2 1   7   4 5 6 7 8 9/9

To Big Daddy —
thanks

THE LIE

One

I woke up that morning suddenly, but a good kind of suddenly, a happy kind. I lay in bed with my arms under my head and stared at the ceiling, supremely contented and at peace with the world. The June sun played notes of light through the blinds, and the warm breeze that feels and smells of summer beat like butterfly wings against the weblike cage of curtains. I woke up that morning knowing it was going to be the best day of my entire life.

I was starting my new job. I was now officially a scoper, which is an excellent thing to be when you live in Ocean City, Maryland, like I do. Scopers are the people who roam the beach during the summer, taking photos of the tourists. They put the photos into these things they call telescopic key rings. You look through the window at one end and see the picture.

1

It may not sound like much, but people are willing to pay a lot for them.

Of course, the best thing about being a scoper was that I would be working for Mark Bishop. I glanced over at my bulletin board where I had pinned up my precious few pictures of him. Mark, the love of my life. Mark with his beat-up Nikes and the little hole in the right one where his little toe peeps out. Mark with his brown hair that curls around his ears and the collar of his shirt, like hands gently cupping the face of someone they love. Mark with his brown eyes that narrow when he's thinking serious thoughts, which is often, because Mark is a pretty bright guy.

I hadn't taken the pictures myself. I didn't have that much nerve. The other photographers from Yearbook had taken them, horsing around like guys do, being goofy. Then they'd thrown them out. I'd saved them from the trash can and taken them home with me, treating them like the treasures they were. Of course, I wish I had taken them myself. I would have done a better job.

There was a knock on the door, and Mom stuck her head in. "Norrie, do you know what time it is? Why are you lying there like that?" she demanded. "Aren't you feeling well?"

"Never better." I smiled cheerfully. "I was just thinking about things, that's all."

"Oh." Mom was not used to me being cheerful in the mornings. She wasn't used to me thinking that early, either. "Well, better get a move on, honey. I've got breakfast waiting downstairs."

I sniffed appreciatively. "Thanks, Mom. I thought I smelled French toast." My mother always makes a special breakfast on first days — first day of school, first day of a job, first day of anything. After the first day, though, you're on your own.

I put on my robe and went downstairs.

"I don't believe it," exclaimed my father, folding his newspaper. "She finally took the camera off her neck. I thought it was glued there permanently."

I poured some juice and sat across from him. "I told you I was wearing it as much as possible to get used to the weight," I said mildly. "It gets heavy after a few hours."

"Don't complain to me, Norrie. We weren't the ones who told you to take this crazy job, lugging that thing around in the hot sun all day — "

"Talking to God knows what kinds of people," Mom added. Dad gave her an approving look, but otherwise didn't miss a beat.

" — and you could have worked in a nice, clean office with air-conditioning," he finished. Dad had gotten me a job at the insurance agency where he works, but I had turned it down. For obvious reasons.

"I'll make more money as a scoper," I said. I had him there. Dad is the practical one. "Maybe I can even start saving for college," I added. My father is always talking about how, even with only one kid, they don't know how they're going to afford to send me to college.

Mom shot a look to defeated Dad. "Just be careful," she said, for maybe the seven-hundredth time. Mom is the worried one. "Don't talk to strange people."

"Mom, it'll be hard not to talk to strange people. How else will I sell any pictures?"

"You know what I mean. Avoid strange-*looking* people. Especially men, Norrie. Don't be so friendly. You never know these days. Ocean City isn't the family place it used to be."

Dad woke up and joined the attack. "How much exactly is Mark going to pay you?" he demanded. "You never did tell us. Is it strictly on commission?"

"The important thing is that I'll be getting valuable work experience," I told him, because I didn't know exactly what the job paid. I'd been so shocked when Mark had asked me, so numb with excitement, so soaring with happiness, that I hadn't really thought of money. "This will look good on my résumé when I try to get a job as a photojournalist."

"Where has all this sudden interest in being a photojournalist come from?" Mom wanted to know. I wasn't about to tell her that it came from Mark, whose goal in life is to jet from one battle zone to another, and who has a tendency to view wars and natural disasters as great photo opportunities.

"You used to like taking nice pictures of animals and children," she complained. "I guess that was too safe for you. Now all you talk about is famine victims and guerrillas. Next you'll be off to Central America and wind up being kidnapped by terrorists!"

"At least she'd make more money doing that than taking pictures of kids and animals, for God's sake," muttered Dad.

I sighed and wolfed down the rest of my French toast. I know my parents love me, and that my mom is overprotective because I'm their only child, and that my dad worries about money because he wants me to be happy and successful, and of course I love them and everything, but they sure do have a way of bringing a person down.

I felt happy again once I got to the boardwalk. On the beach some kids were flying kites. One was bright yellow and orange; you could see the colors even though the kite was way, way up, past the sea gulls, almost to the clouds, shining down like another sun. It seemed to follow me as I made my way down the boardwalk to where Mark and I had agreed to meet.

He was there ahead of me. I could see the halo of light shining on his beautiful hair, picking out coppery glints among the brown, and I felt my heart move inside my chest, doing that familiar little flip-flop.

He was leaning nonchalantly against the railing, drinking coffee, looking so mature and sophisticated that I almost cried from the sheer beauty of him. It was like looking at a sculpture by Michelangelo or a painting by Leonardo da Vinci or something like that, and saying to yourself, "It's so beautiful, it can't be real." That's the way I felt about Mark.

"Hi," I greeted him, breathless. "I'm sorry I'm late. I hope you haven't been waiting long."

He shook his head, throwing his cup into a trash can. "You're not late; I'm early. I was up anyway to do some shooting — wanted to catch the early morning light." He glanced down at me, appreciatively, I think. I was wearing white shorts and a striped red top. The shorts were a little too tight, and I figured that worked to my advantage. My legs are pretty decent.

"Listen, thanks again for offering me this job," I

5

told him all in a rush. I was always nervous around Mark; this was something that was going to have to change. "You won't regret it, I swear. I really appreciate the opportunity."

"Well, to be honest, I asked Jeff Johnson first, but he already had a job lined up as a lifeguard. I figured you, being what? — fourteen?"

"Fifteen!" I corrected him, feeling my face go red. "I've been fifteen for *months*."

"Well, anyway, I figured you could use the job, and it's really not that much different from what you've been doing all semester in Yearbook. Shooting groups, getting them to smile, clowning around, you know. Nothing artsy or creative, so you won't have to worry about that."

"Oh. Well, I really do appreciate you thinking of me."

"Hey, you're doing me a favor. It's gotten too much for me to handle alone. And I've got this photo exhibit at Bowman's Art Gallery at the end of the summer to prepare for. I'll need lots of daylight hours to do my work."

I nodded. Everybody at school knew Mark had been chosen to exhibit at a professional gallery, not as a student, but as a representative Ocean City artist. Impressive, huh? His photographs were going to be on sale and everything.

After that, I couldn't think of anything to say, and I knew it would be totally dweeby to thank him yet again. There was a short pause.

"So, here we are," he said. "All set?"

I held up my camera. "Whenever you are!"

He started to explain the routine to me, and I lis-

6

tened as carefully as I could. I didn't want to screw up and have him thinking I was some kind of idiot.

"Your territory will be from here to 19th Street," he told me. "When things get more crowded, after July fourth, you won't have to cover so much, but for now try to get everyone from here to 19th Street, okay?"

"No problem," I replied.

"You want to concentrate on families with kids, and groups of girls — they're the ones who buy the most," he continued. "Take about three times the number of shots as there are people in the group — never less than ten or twelve at a time. If it's a group of girls, each one will want her own. If it's a family, they'll want to send some to Grandma, and so forth. And some they won't like, so don't be too stingy with your film. Got it?"

"No problem," I repeated.

"Okay, so after you've taken all you need, tell them they can pick them up that evening after seven P.M. at Thompson's. You've got the cards with Thompson's address that I gave you the other day?"

I nodded and patted my camera bag. Thompson's is where we got the film developed, and where the customers went to choose their photos and pick up their key rings. Thompson's, Mark explained to me, are the ones who really make the money, because they are the ones who own the concession.

"Great, get them out, and we'll hit a few groups so I can show you how it's done." He looked out on the beach. It was still early in the day, and still early in the season, but there were already enough people there to keep us busy for hours.

"So tell me, where should we go first?" he asked, testing me. But I was ready.

"How about the couple with the two toddlers? See them?" I pointed with my camera. "The two little blond boys playing with a shovel and pail."

"Good choice." He nodded and smiled. God, what a smile! "Come on," he said. "Let's go."

The parents of the two little boys were pathetically eager for Mark to take their pictures, of course. We grouped the boys alone, then with Dad, then with Mom, then all four of them together. Then one of the little angels reached over and began to pull his brother's hair out, and all hell broke loose. It nearly ruined everything, but I think we got away with at least six good pictures.

"They'll buy every one," predicted Mark. "Who next?"

I didn't have a chance to answer, because just then a girl called to him, "Hey, are you a photographer?"

Mark turned around slowly and flashed the girl and her friends those incredible dimples of his. Mark has the deepest dimples I've ever seen. How deep are they? They're so deep, you could boil an egg in them, that's how deep they are.

No female alive can resist those dimples. The girls broke into fits of giggles. Totally uncool. Definitely seventh-graders.

"Sure am," he said. "Would you girls like your pictures taken? A little souvenir of Ocean City. You could give them to your boyfriends."

More giggles. Then the boldest girl straightened herself up, glanced at me, and said in this disgustingly coy voice, "I don't have a boyfriend right now."

Mark made a noise of disbelief. "What? — the boys at your school are all blind? Or maybe they've just never seen you in that skimpy suit with a really great tan. How about a picture — show them what they've been missing?"

That got them, of course. By this time the girls were positively palpitating. There were four of them; each wanted an individual shot, then group shots, then paired shots. It added up to a lot of sales.

Mark talked to them the entire time he was shooting, stuff like, "No, Mindy, don't sit cross-legged, stretch your legs out — there you go, *much* sexier!" and, "Jenny, pull your hair forward, and take your sunglasses off — let's see those beautiful eyes!"

As much as I love Mark, it was enough to make me want to gag.

"They really fell for that crap!" I said when we were out of earshot. Not that I blamed them, of course; I would have, too, when I was their age. Come to think of it, I still would, if it were Mark saying those things.

"Don't knock it, it works," he replied, smiling. "Think you can do better?"

That sounded like a dare to me. I never, ever refuse a dare. And I figured it might be fun to show him that I'm not exactly a dog with the opposite sex myself.

"Wait here," I told him and sauntered over to where a group of boys about my own age were sitting on the beach, horsing around.

They stopped when I approached them. "Hi there," I said in a very friendly manner. "Would you guys like your picture taken? It makes a nice key ring."

"Nah, those things are for girls," said a sandy-haired

one. The way he said *girls* let me know he wasn't exactly the sensitive Phil Donahue type.

"You could give them to your girlfriends," I suggested. "It makes a nice souvenir."

They all looked at each other warily. They didn't have girlfriends, but, unlike the girls, they weren't about to admit it. "Or you could give it to the girl you meet here," I said. "It would be like a reminder for her when you've gone back home."

"I haven't met any girls here yet," said a scrawny, dark-haired boy. You never will, either, I thought, and gave him a pretty sexy smile. Not my sexiest smile, you understand, but close enough.

"You will," I told him. "So what do you guys say?"

"How much?"

God, this was getting *humiliating*. I couldn't help but remember that the girls hadn't asked Mark the cost until after he'd already taken the shots.

After a lot of hemming and hawing, they finally agreed. I lined them up and starting shooting, but they seemed to be more interested in being jerks than getting their pictures taken. When I went back to Mark, he was standing with his arms folded across his chest, grinning.

"Not exactly the shy type, are you?"

"I was just following the example set by my teacher," I said nonchalantly.

"Yeah, I noticed you're a fast learner. Too bad it doesn't work so well with boys."

"What do you mean?"

He moved his hands expressively. "Just this. Those yahoos won't come to pick them up. *You* maybe they'd come to pick up, but the pictures — " He stopped and shook his head.

Inside, I was so thrilled that I could die. So he *did* notice! Outside, I stayed cool. Very, very cool.

"Wanna bet?" I challenged.

"Sure."

"Okay. Breakfast on me if you're right."

"You're on."

I held out my hand and he took it. Instantly I felt hundreds of electric jolts speed through my body, making a beeline straight for my heart. I swear to God, if I'd been an electrical appliance I would have short-circuited.

His skin was warm, and his grasp firm, just like a man's should be. As he let go of my hand, my fingers just barely registered the soft fuzz of blond hair above his knuckles. Mark has magnificent hands; artist's hands, the fingers long and well-developed. It must come from working with them so much, creating all those beautiful pictures. I never realized before how important a person's hand can be, but now I know it really says a lot about his character. I loved what Mark's hand said about him. I loved what Mark's hand did to me.

"Ready for some more?" he asked, and I nodded my head wordlessly. Unfortunately, Mark was talking about taking pictures, and not about more physical contact. That all-too-brief handshake had turned me into a jujube, but it hadn't seemed to move him at all.

Just you wait, Mark Christopher Bishop, I vowed, my heart turning over as that gorgeous brown head swung away from me. *Someday it will. Just you wait.*

• • •

Mark was right about the pictures. Those jerky boys didn't come by to pick them up. When I went by Thompson's that evening, they were still there, in their little telescopes, unclaimed, unwanted. Of course, the ones of the giggling seventh-graders were all gone. Every single one.

"Relax," said Joe, the assistant manager. "You can't sell them all."

That was easy for him to say — he wasn't working on commission. Not that I really minded; actually, I was pretty happy he hadn't sold those particular ones. I now had a breakfast date for the next morning.

"Mark been in yet?" I asked him casually.

"He was, earlier. To drop his film off."

"Right." I nodded. "Do you think he'll be back today?"

He shook his head. "Nah. I doubt it."

"Well, what time does he usually come in?" I persisted.

Joe scratched his chin. Joe has a permanent three-day stubble on his chin, which looks kind of weird because the rest of his face is very smooth and white.

"He doesn't have a set time that I know of," he finally said. "You got a problem with the Nikon? Maybe I can help."

"No, that's okay, it's nothing. I just wanted . . . uh, to ask him something about work. I'll talk to him tomorrow." I backed toward the door. "See you!"

TWO

Mark and I had arranged to meet at ten the next morning on the boardwalk. I arrived early because I wanted to talk to Brenda, who works at Frank's Fries. Brenda's been my best friend since fifth grade.

She was already behind the booth, scrubbing the oil vats like her life depended upon it. As if any amount of scrubbing could ever get that grease off!

A loose strand of hair had escaped her white cap and looked like it was getting in her eyes, but she didn't seem to notice. She kept on applying the elbow grease, her tongue peeking out on one side of her mouth in concentration. I knew she would make a good subject, so I took out my camera and started shooting.

I had taken at least seven shots before the boy working next to her noticed me and nudged her.

"Norrie!" she shrieked, holding her hand up to shield her face. "What are you doing?"

"Getting some candid shots of the working girl."

"No fair! You might have warned me!"

"Then they wouldn't be candid. Come on, Bren, put your hand down. I'm only practicing."

"Well, practice on someone else," she retorted. "I look like doggie-do in this uniform, and I don't appreciate you recording it for posterity."

Attractive people in attractive clothes don't always make the most interesting photographs, but I didn't tell Brenda this. She is super-sensitive and doesn't like her looks. Which is ridiculous, because she is really cute, even if the uniform sucked the big one.

"How's the job going so far?" I asked.

She groaned and made an angry swipe at the counter. "Unhealthy. Don't you think standing over a hot fryer all day, breathing in all those fumes, is going to stunt my growth? And it's so filthy! When I get home at night, I practically have to take the grease off with a crowbar."

"Sick of fries yet?" I asked her sympathetically. Brenda claimed she only took the job to cure her of her intense love of French fries. Brenda's a bit on the plump side.

"But definitely," she replied. "Just the smell of them makes me want to throw up."

"So it worked! Hey, maybe I should get a job at the fudge factory," I told her. "I'd like to be sick of chocolate."

"Nobody could ever get sick of chocolate, Norrie. That's impossible. And you've already got a great job.

Oh — wait a minute! I almost forgot. Today's your first date with Mark!"

"Well, it's not really a date," I demurred. "I asked him, you know."

"It involves a meal, together, and by yourselves, doesn't it? You've painted your fingernails *and* your toenails. I like the pink, by the way. I'm glad you didn't go with the apricot; it was really putrid. So it's definitely a date. You don't color-coordinate your toes and fingers for someone who isn't a date." She announced this last part with authority and then sighed. "I'll bet by the end of summer, you'll be the most solid couple ever."

Now you know why Brenda has been my best friend since the fifth grade. Sometimes she knows exactly the right thing to say.

"I have to tell you, I was starting to get worried," she said, rubbing the vats again. "I kept wondering if it was worth it. Don't get offended or anything, but all those months and months of obsessing about him! And all those crazy stunts you pulled!"

Unfortunately, Brenda doesn't *always* say exactly the right thing.

"Come on, Bren, they weren't *that* crazy."

"Well, I guess that depends on your definition of crazy. What about the time you got your sweater hooked on his notebook binder?"

I sighed, thinking about that little white sweater that had given its life so that I could have a chance to get closer to Mark. It was a great sweater, too, always falling off my shoulder in a very sexy way. Now it had a big hole in the sleeve.

"Okay, it's true that didn't turn out like I'd hoped," I conceded. Mark had barely glanced at me while working that sweater out. I'd apologized, even though it was *my* sweater he'd just put a hole in, and he'd sort of smiled at me in this absentminded way. I'd sacrificed that sweater for a smile that wasn't even *there*.

"And what about the time you bicycled by the park where Mark *just happened* to be playing tennis, and you *just happened* to walk by his court with your bike, which *just happened* to have a busted chain?" Brenda asked. "Don't you think breaking your own bike might qualify as just a *teeny* bit crazy?"

I'd gotten that idea from my cousin Steffie, who is just about the person I most admire in the world. When it comes to getting guys, she not only knows every trick in the book, she wrote the book, if you know what I mean. No kidding, there has never been a guy she couldn't get, and that includes her husband, who is so totally fine, he'd make a Greek god look like a geek in marble.

Anyway, once, back in her single days, when Steff was after some guy, she'd gotten her car to break down in front of his house. I don't know how she'd managed this feat, but it worked. He'd come out of the house, helped her with her car, and fallen in love. She said it had brought out his protective male instincts. I say one look at gorgeous Steffie brought out all his protective male *lust*. Not that I would have minded a little lust on Mark's part, of course.

I didn't have a car, couldn't drive one if I did, but I did have a bicycle. I'd figured that would work just as well. It didn't. Mark's partner — a very nice guy — came over to help me, while Mark rode off in a little red car driven by another one of his blondes. He'd waved at us as they passed; the blonde had tooted the horn. Let me tell you, that was a day that will live in infamy.

"I wish you would stop reminding me of all my failures," I complained. "Don't rain on my parade, you know? Besides, something I did sure paid off, or else I wouldn't be where I am now, right?"

"But definitely," Brenda agreed. "It was taking up photography that did it. I guess it was worth the sacrifice, right?"

By that she was referring to joining Yearbook. I'd had to take a photography class first to learn how to take pictures. Boring, but I was nothing if not determined. I mean, I'd checked out photography books from the library and even *read* them, that's how determined I was. Plus, I'd had to give up what I really wanted last Christmas — a hunter green suede jacket I'd had my eyes on for months — so that my parents would get me a super-duper Nikon instead.

Taking up photography had been Steffie's suggestion. That and wearing short skirts. She was the one who told me my legs are pretty decent.

"Yeah, it was worth it," I agreed. "Yearbook was a lot of fun. And I think this would be a great job even without Mark."

"Speaking of the boss man," Bren said, gesturing to the boardwalk, "here he comes now. Looking very very, but definitely."

I turned and saw Mark walking toward us. He was wearing cutoffs and his familiar white Nikes. Gorgeous.

"Good luck, Norrie," Brenda called. "Stop by later, okay?"

I waved back at her. She gave me a thumbs-up signal.

Mark hadn't seen me yet, and I realized this was my chance to add to my photo collection. I ducked behind a lamppost and started shooting; the light was perfect, and I know I got some great shots before he spotted me. But he didn't hold his hand up like Brenda had. He didn't seem at all self-conscious.

"I hope that's your own film you're using," he said, grinning.

"It is."

"So, what gives? You thinking of becoming a member of the paparazzi?"

I shrugged, putting my camera down. "Well, they say the money's good. What do you think? Am I ready for the *National Enquirer*?"

"Gee, I don't know," he said with mock seriousness. "Think you can handle all that prestige?"

"Just as long as I don't have to take pictures of two-headed babies and people possessed by aliens," I said. "I have my standards, you know."

He laughed at that, and if I thought the sun was bright before, it was practically blinding me now. You're doing great, I told myself, keep it up, keep it up. . . .

"I owe you a breakfast," I told him. He looked puzzled, so I added, "The bet, remember? You were right, those jerks never did come to pick up their pictures." I smiled ruefully, trying to look very mature and good-natured in my defeat.

"Tough luck," he agreed. "But I won't hold you to the breakfast. I already ate."

I was really sorry to hear that, especially since I hadn't. "Coffee, then?" I nodded to the folder he had

18

in his hand. "It'll be easier to show me what I did wrong if we're sitting down, anyway."

So I settled for a croissant and a diet Coke, while Mark drank his coffee. I was getting too nervous to eat very much, anyway, even though I was hungry. It was really weird — hungry and slightly nauseous at the same time.

Mark laid out some of the photos I'd taken the day before — ones people hadn't bought — and started pointing out what was wrong with them.

"Remember to concentrate on *faces*," he said earnestly. "Especially when they're women who act like they think they're fat." He pointed to one woman who looked like a poster child for Overeaters Anonymous. "Technically speaking, this is not a bad photograph," he continued. "But you've got to remember, Norrie, that people only want to buy photos where they look good. It's your job to *make* them look good, even if you haven't got a lot to work with. It's not up to us to point out the truth to these people. Let them have their illusions."

I nodded. Mark was so nice, so sensitive, and what he said made a lot of sense. Who needs a truthful photographer? That's what mirrors are for.

He smiled and handed me the photos. "But, basically, you're doing okay. I don't think we need to work together again, do you?"

That was a tough one. On the one hand, I wanted to be with him every moment I could. On the other hand, I didn't want him to think I was so slow that he'd regret hiring me.

"I guess not," I agreed reluctantly. "But you will be working the beach today, right?"

19

"Sure."

"Great! Maybe we'll run into each other."

He shook his head. "No, we don't want to overlap. You stay in your territory, I'll stay in mine. The next time you see me will probably be when I give you your money. Oh, and if you've got a problem you can't handle on your own, you can call me, of course." He must have noticed my crestfallen expression, because he gave me a reassuring pat on the shoulder. "Hey, don't sweat it. You'll do fine on your own. No kidding."

I tried a smile, but my lips couldn't seem to make the right movement. Not see each other till payday? Was he outa his gourd, or what? Why else had I taken this job?

"Uh — maybe we could meet later," I suggested. "I might still have some questions after today." I tried to smile again. This time my lips worked. "Maybe I could buy you an ice cream. I still feel kind of guilty about ducking out on breakfast, no matter what you say."

"Hey, it wasn't a real bet," he said, looking surprised. "Can't make it today, though, or I'd take you up on it. I've got something else planned."

And I knew what that "something else" was: a girl. I could tell just by the look in his eyes that it was a girl. I could practically *smell* that it was a girl. And the girl sure as heck wasn't me.

Mark was right about one thing. We didn't run into each other all day, even though I stayed pretty close to the line that separated his territory from mine.

I was so distracted, keeping an eye out for him, that I must have asked the same couple three times if they wanted their picture taken. The woman finally got so fed up with me that she yelled in this loud, screeching voice that you could have heard all the way to Delaware, "For the *last time* — No! No! No! We do *not* want one of those damned key rings!"

After that, I made sure I stayed clear of her. Some people have no sympathy.

"I'm sure it's not as bad as you think," Brenda said sympathetically. I could always count on Brenda for sympathy. "You don't even know for sure that it was a girl. He didn't actually mention one, did he?"

"Brenda, a woman knows these things." I sighed and took another bite of pizza. "Face it, he'll be a senior this year and he can have practically any girl he wants. To him I'm just a kid who works for him. Otherwise, the guy doesn't even know I'm alive."

"Oh, no, that's not true, Norrie."

I noticed she didn't sound very convinced. Brenda's a good friend, but not such a good liar.

"You're right," I said bleakly. "He knows I'm alive, he just doesn't care. I swear to God, Brenda, I think I could stand in front of Mark stark *naked*, doing an erotic mating dance guaranteed to give all *normal* men within a thirty-mile radius a major case of hormone overdrive — you know, like those green women on that episode of the old *Star Trek*? Remember?"

Brenda nodded her head. "I remember. Supposedly no man could resist them, even if they were painted putrid green."

"Mark could," I said savagely. "Mark would only notice if he thought it would make a good photo."

There was a silence, and then I caught her look. Suddenly we both broke out in fits of giggles. I mean, it *was* funny. The whole thing was so ridiculous, it couldn't help but be funny, even for me.

"Oh, God," said Brenda.

"You've got sauce on your chin," I told her, still laughing. She wasn't. She was staring behind me, openmouthed.

"Don't turn around — " she began, but it was too late. I looked just in time to see Mark and Leeza Harrow walk in hand in hand.

"Leeza the Sleeza of the junior class," Brenda exclaimed scornfully, glancing at me. "I'm sure it's nothing serious, Norrie. He can't really like *her*."

I didn't answer her. I was looking at the love of my life holding Leeza Harrow's hand. She was pretty, in a cheap kind of way, with tight clothes and really big hair. The hair was blonde, of course. It always was. Mark has a thing for blondes. I am not a blonde, in case you haven't guessed. My hair is dull and ordinary and brown.

"He can't really like her," Bren repeated. "She's *flat-chested*."

Brenda may be a teeny bit on the plump side, but she is definitely not flat-chested. Neither am I. But I'm the one staring at Mark like a lovesick puppy, and Leeza's the one holding his hand, so just how important are boobs, anyway?

Leeza and Mark, slices in hand, were moving toward the door. I turned to Brenda and smiled cheerfully. "Your break must be over by now. We'd better get going."

"Norrie, you're not going to do something stupid like follow them, are you?"

"Get real, Bren. That is so junior high."

• • •

You get real, Norrie Plimmon, I was saying to myself ten minutes later, while hiding behind a rack of T-shirts that boldly announced to the world, "I'm horny." This is as low as a person can get, I thought. Norrie Plimmon, you have sunk to the bottom of the pit.

Mark and Leeza moved toward the cash register. I ducked my head so they wouldn't see me.

So, by now you're probably asking yourself, is this girl mental or what? Is any guy worth this kind of aggravation? The answer is, of course, no. But I couldn't seem to help myself.

Mark was paying for a sun visor. He handed it to Leeza. She gave him a big kiss. I think she even put some tongue into it. The Sleeza! She was so totally gross! Couldn't Mark see that?

But Mark was blind, that much I knew. He was so blind, he didn't realize that I'd been in love with him since my very first day of high school. That was September, now it was June — nine months ago. Nine months, one week, six days, four hours, and twenty minutes, to be exact.

It happened during freshmen assembly. Mark had been there taking photos for the Yearbook. This was before I knew that photography is sort of an obsession with him, before I knew anything about him at all. All I knew at that moment was that I was seriously in love. That's the God's honest truth. I saw him across the crowded auditorium, his face partially hidden by his camera, the flash popping out over a hundred or so nervous, pimply freshmen, and I *knew*. I fell completely, totally, and irrevocably in love.

23

Unfortunately, Mark didn't. This is what they call unrequited love. It's what I call the absolute pits. I wouldn't wish a case of unrequited love on my worst enemy, who, at that moment, appeared to be Leeza.

Right now she was pawing him like he was her personal bag of Kibbles 'n Bits. I was watching, the way you worry a loose tooth with your tongue, testing to see if it still hurt. It did.

They moved back outside to the boardwalk. I followed, sticking close to the store side, where the people were, my head bobbing up and down so I could see them but they wouldn't see me.

Let me just say here and now that I am not totally repulsive-looking. For the record, I'm not really so bad-looking at all. Some people, believe it or not, might even go so far as to say I'm kind of pretty.

I'm not stupid. And I've got a good personality. Gutsy, Brenda calls me. Isn't gutsy sort of a synonym for proud? So where was my so-called pride now?

The bad thing about my looks is that my eyes are two different colors. It's not as weird as it sounds, at least I don't think it is. You don't even notice at first, but when you get up close you can see that one is hazel, and the other is green.

I read once that they used to burn girls with eyes like mine as witches. They thought it was the sure sign of the devil. Sometimes, like right at that moment, I wished I were a witch. I'd mix up a love potion for Mark and put a curse on all skinny blondes.

With that last thought I let Mark and Leeza the Sleeza walk ahead, unchaperoned, unaccompanied, but not unwatched. My eyes stayed with them, keyed on Leeza's bony shoulders jutting like teeth from the jaws of her neon-pink stretch top. My two-colored eyes didn't let them go until the neon-pink was just a dot, then not even a dot, and the two of them, happily oblivious, were swallowed up by the crowd.

I walked back on the boardwalk to my side of the beach.

Three

"Brenda, I have done everything humanly possible to get this guy's attention, and *nothing* has worked," I was saying angrily several hours later while we sat at a booth at McDonald's. "How long can a person beat her head against the wall before she says 'hey! that hurts'?" I demanded. "I mean, just how much is a person supposed to take?"

"Gee, Norrie, I don't know — "

"This much, Bren. I mean, this is *it*. This is where I say 'no more.' The end, I quit, I *give up*." I squashed a Styrofoam container with my fist for emphasis. "I tell you, I've had it with that guy! I hope he goes swimming with one of his blondes, gets caught in the undertow, and *dies*, that's what I hope."

"Don't say that," Brenda said, eyeing my hands before pushing her tray out of my reach. "What if he really did die — think how you would feel!"

"Okay, fine, I don't hope he dies. I just hope he gets paralyzed."

"For life?" she squeaked. "That's worse!"

I shrugged. "Back to death, then. I liked it better, anyway."

"Maybe he'll get hit by lightning," she suggested. "You know, shake him up a little. Make him realize you're the only one for him."

"At the rate I'm going, it would take a couple of megatons of lightning," I replied. "No, that's it. I'm finished. I give up. I know when I'm licked, for Chrissake."

For a few seconds the only sound was Brenda slurping on her chocolate shake. Brenda always likes to get every last drop. Then, "Do you really mean it, Norrie?"

"No." I sighed. "No, of course I don't mean it. Do I ever?"

Brenda, true friend that she is, sighed with me. She'd done her best all evening to cheer me up, and I hadn't helped much. First we'd gone to see the new Tom Cruise movie. I'd always thought Mark looked a little like Tom Cruise, with his dimples and all, but sitting in the darkened theater, I'd suddenly realized that Mark looked a lot more like him than I'd originally thought. Now I see that he could definitely be a younger brother. Brenda didn't agree at first, but eventually she saw it my way.

Then we'd come to McDonald's and devoured two fish fillet sandwiches each. Brenda and I are the only people I've ever met who actually get the fish fillet sandwiches at McDonald's. We don't get French fries anymore, even though I used to love them. After what Brenda told me about how they make fries at Frank's Fries, and how they aren't too careful to be clean and how they sometimes drop them on the floor and put them right back into the fryer, well, I just didn't think I'd ever be able to eat French fries again.

And, now, of course, we were talking about my nonexistent love life. Truly a night to remember.

"School will be starting up in a few months, and my one chance to get him will be gone. I'll never be able to compete with the senior girls," I said, feeling my old buddy Despair creeping up on me. "I swear to God, Bren, somehow, someway, I've just got to get through to him before the end of summer."

Brenda nodded sympathetically and placed her milk shake back on the table. Otherwise, she said nothing.

"Any ideas?" I prodded. Talk about the blind leading the blind!

She hesitated, darting a glance at the table catty-corner to us. I couldn't see them, but I knew boys were sitting there. I could tell by the way she lowered her voice.

"How about going out with another guy?"

"You mean, try to make him jealous?" I frowned. "My cousin Steffie suggested that to me once, but it seems kind of sleazy, doesn't it? Still," I said doubtfully, "you never know, it might work. I'm just about ready to try anything."

Bren cleared her throat the way she does when she's about to say something important. I waited. Maybe she had an idea I hadn't thought of yet. "I didn't mean go out with other guys to make Mark jealous," she said slowly. "I meant to just *go out with other guys*. You know, just to have some fun, maybe get a new perspective on things."

I looked at her, stunned. I couldn't believe Bren was turning traitor on me now, when I really needed her the most. "But you said taking this job was a great way to get together with Mark," I protested. "You said we'd be a solid couple by September. What happened to make you change your mind?"

"I haven't exactly changed my mind," she said. "I've always thought you shouldn't cut yourself off from other . . . opportunities. Why not go out with someone else — why should you live like a nun? There are a lot of boys who would *just love* to go out with you."

"I don't want other boys. I want Mark. I happen to be in love with him, in case you've forgotten."

"No chance of that," she said, sighing. "But you won't always be, will you? Don't you think we're a little young to be falling in love forever?"

"Maybe *you* are."

"Come on, Norrie, you're only five months older than me."

"Well, those must be five very important months, because I know for a fact that I am not too young. Juliet was younger than me when she fell in love with Romeo, you know."

"Yeah, and look how that turned out," she said darkly.

I glared at her. "Brenda, you're supposed to be making me feel better."

"Sorry."

But she didn't look it. I started shredding my napkin, not answering her.

"You asked me for my opinion," Brenda reminded me.

"No, I didn't."

"Are you mad?" Brenda's always thinking people are mad at her.

"No, Bren, I know you're trying to help. Look," I said, trying to explain to her how I felt, "I'd give him up in a minute if I could. Believe me, I would. But I can't. I tell you, I'm crazy in love with the guy. Anyway, I can't give up now, not when I'm at least working with him, can I?"

"No one said you should give him up. But there's no harm in just *talking* to another boy, is there?" She took another furtive glance at the table to the side of us. "Like those two boys over there," she whispered. "The dark-haired one has been really *staring* at you, Norrie. No — don't look!"

But, of course, I looked anyway. One glance at their burnt noses and Ocean City T-shirts was enough. I turned back to Brenda, who was squirming in her seat. "Tourists," I said with disgust. "No, thanks."

"Well, *I* think they're cute."

"Great, then you go talk to them," I said, and was sorry for it when I saw the look on Bren's face. She would never have the nerve to talk to a guy she didn't know. She didn't have the nerve to talk to guys she *did* know.

Suddenly I felt like a real bitch, remembering that Bren had patiently listened to me all evening, all year, if you want to get down to it, and here I was giving her a hard time. She was only trying to help. She was totally wrong, of course, because she didn't know *squat* about being in love. But at least she tried. She was the best best friend a person could ever have.

My best best friend, meanwhile, was still giving the two guys the once-over out of the corner of her eye. "Want me to get them over here?" I asked her.

Her eyes widened, and she started shaking her head. "No, Norrie, don't you dare — "

It was too late; I could tell she didn't mean it. What are best friends for? I turned my head slowly and gave the dark-haired one a smile. A *very special* smile, like the one I'd given those boys on the beach, with a little something extra added.

That was all it took. Not that I'm so drop-dead gorgeous, you understand, but you could tell these guys were desperate for something to do, for someone to talk to, maybe for something a little more. They must have thought they'd struck gold with Brenda and me.

The dark-haired one was from Pennsylvania, but the other one had just moved to O.C. I concentrated on the dark one, and left the local for Brenda.

So we talked and laughed, drank Coke until I thought I was going to float away, and talked and laughed some more. Even Bren got into it; she was still a little pink from blushing, but she was also making an obvious effort not to be so shy.

I was glad Bren was having a good time, but I couldn't help wishing it were Mark giving me admiring looks across the table instead of this dark-haired guy from Pennsylvania. If I couldn't have that, I wished that Mark would come in and see this dark-haired guy giving me admiring looks. Fat chance of that happening. Right now Mark was probably with Leeza the Sleeza. I'm sure he had bigger and better things planned than dinner at McDonald's.

The guys were pretty disappointed when we had to leave; it was almost like they thought we'd cheated them or something. Brenda's took her phone number; I told mine not to bother since he was leaving soon and I was too busy to see him during the next two days. I guess he got the message.

Brenda and I giggled all the way home — I swear, we were acting just like a pair of seventh-graders. We were laughing so hard, our sides started to ache.

"God, did you see the looks on their faces when we told them we had to go?" asked Brenda, between breaths. "It was pitiful!"

"Yeah, I guess we broke their hearts," I said breezily. "Better luck next time, guys!"

"But they sure were cute." Brenda sighed. "Didn't you think so?"

"I think Peter thought *you* were cute," I replied. "He seemed nice, too."

"Yeah, he *was* nice, wasn't he?" She smiled happily. "You know, it's too bad you only have eyes for Mark, 'cause I could tell that guy Chuck really liked you."

I was about to tell her that Chuckie-boy would have liked *anything* that was female and breathed, but I remembered what Mark had said about not disillusioning people. What she said next made me glad I had kept my mouth shut.

"God, Peter is such a babe! Do you think he'll really call me?"

"Of course!" I said loyally. "But he'd better hurry, before somebody else moves in! I bet you'll meet lots of boys this summer, working on the boardwalk, right in the heat of things."

"Heat is right," she said, making a face. "They're not exactly banging down my door, in case you haven't noticed."

I put my arm around her shoulder. "Come on, Bren, don't talk that way. You're cute, and sweet, and *lots* of boys like you. All you need is a little more confidence. That's all it takes!"

Bren shook her head, sighing again. "I'll never have half your nerve. To just go up and talk to a guy, and that look you gave them tonight — *that* took guts! I don't know how you do it, Norrie."

I shrugged, thinking how hard it was for me with Mark. "It's easy when you don't care," I told her. "That's the secret. Not to care."

The days dragged on. I did my job and kept an eye on Mark. Leeza Harrow didn't hold on to him for very long; I mean, the girl had no staying power whatsoever. She was followed by a seemingly endless supply of blonde tourists. Okay, so maybe that's a slight exaggeration. I still say two blonde out-of-towners in one lousy week sets a definite pattern.

Let me just say here and now that Norrie Plimmon is no quitter. Like my first-grade teacher wrote on my very first report card, "Norrie has tremendous perseverance. She always finishes what she starts." Mrs. Kilpatrick, bless her, knew her stuff. I never, ever give up. Never.

But, quite honestly, nine months, two weeks, four days, and fifteen hours of constant defeat was really starting to get to me. I figured by now I deserved some sort of medal for perseverance. Quick! Call Ripley's Believe It or Not!

I had thought briefly of going into a decline — you know, like one of those Victorian heroines. But that's just too boring, and I get too hungry. Besides, I'm basically a person of action. I can't just sit around; I have to do *something*.

So then I decided to fight fire with fire. I started flirting like mad with the nearest male handy whenever Mark was around. Mark didn't notice, which was why I was in my room, moping and listening to slow, sad music.

There was a quick rap on the door, then the sweet, melodious strains of my father's voice. "Norrie! Turn that damned racket off! Time for dinner!"

I grunted my reply, rolling over on the bed to switch off my stereo. It was a good thing I'd decided not to go into a decline. I could smell my mother's oven-fried chicken.

I ate three pieces. My parents were arguing about what movie they were going to see that night. Dad wanted a major blockbuster with plenty of action (that's where I get it from, I guess), while Mom was holding out for one of those artsy, unprofitable films. Mom won this round. Then they asked me if I wanted to go with them.

"No, those movies you like are so boring, Mom. Like the last one. A group of middle-aged women sit in trendy New York restaurants and bitch about men. I mean, they were witty and all that, but that stuff gets old pretty fast."

"Watch your language," growled my father. He can

swear like a Marine whenever he wants, but I can't even use a perfectly acceptable verb like "to bitch."

"It's funny you should think that's boring, when that's exactly what you and Brenda spend ninety percent of your time doing," Mom replied. "You and she have more in common with the women in that movie than you think."

"Mom, when was the last time you heard me talk about my biological time clock?"

"Well, that you don't do, thank God," she conceded. "But you and Brenda do complain a lot about boys. You just do it while eating at Burger King instead of at a sushi bar."

"I hate Burger King; they only serve Pepsi," I said, but suddenly got this very bad feeling that Mom was right. Bren and I did spend a lot of time eating and sitting around in fast-food places. And we did discuss every minute detail of our every interaction with the opposite sex. Was I really that boring? Was that why I couldn't get anywhere with Mark?

What a depressing thought. A fifteen-year-old, no matter how mature for her age, which I was, should never let herself be compared to a bunch of crabby women in their thirties.

Maybe I needed to broaden my horizons. I could start reading the newspaper more often, listen to different kinds of music. Maybe I needed to work on being a more interesting person.

The phone rang. I leapt up, hoping it was Brenda, so I could share this revelation with her. We could start making plans together. This could be our summer of self-improvement.

"For once I would like to finish dinner without the phone ringing," complained my father. "If it's Brenda, tell her you'll call her back."

Of course, if it was for him, he'd talk just as long as he pleased. Fathers never obey any of their own rules. I picked up the phone.

"Norrie!" Brenda squealed into the receiver. "Guess! Guess what happened?"

"What?"

"Guess! You'll never guess, but guess anyway. Guess who called me?"

"Who?"

"Guess who called me and wants to go out with me? *Me!* Guess!"

"When? Who called you?" I demanded. "Someone from school?"

"God, not those dorks," she said disdainfully. "Oh, never mind, you'll never guess in a million years. It was *Peter!* Can you believe it? Remember, from McDonald's?"

"Really?"

"Yes!"

"Really? He called you?"

"Really! He said he'd been wanting to do it all week, but he didn't have the nerve. Can you believe it? *He* didn't have the nerve?"

Peter had been the shy one, so actually, I could believe that part. "But, Bren, this is great!" I told her excitedly. "Really great!"

"He also said he had to wait until his cousin left, because his cousin was really miffed that you wouldn't give him your phone number," she added, with just a tinge of disapproval. "Oh, if only you had! Then we could have gone out together! OH, GOD!" she shrieked. "Do you realize I have to go out with him *alone*? Norrie! You have to help me! What am I going to say to him? What am I going to *wear*?"

"Don't worry, you'll do fine. You had plenty to say to each other the other night, didn't you?"

" 'Don't worry'? It's less than twenty-four hours away, and I'm already a nervous wreck! Can you come over after dinner?" she begged. "Please, Norrie, I really need your help. I don't even know what I'm going to do to my hair!"

"Let me ask." I held the receiver against my chest. "Mom!" I called. "Can I go over to Brenda's after dinner?"

"Yes, we'll drop you off on our way to the movies. But get off that phone *this minute*."

"No problem," I told Brenda. "But I have to finish eating now."

"All right!" she screamed. "See you later!"

I put the receiver back in its cradle and stared at it. Brenda had a date!

"What's wrong?" Dad asked when I came back to the table. "One of your boy-crazy schemes didn't work? Do the two of you need to regroup for the next battle?"

I made a face at him. My dad always teases me about being boy-crazy, which I hadn't been for a long time, since Mark was certainly not a boy. "As a matter of fact," I replied with great dignity, "a very nice guy asked Brenda out. She wants me to go over to help her decide what to wear."

"So why so glum?" asked Mom.

"I'm not glum," I told her. "I'm happy for her. Really happy. Peter's a really nice guy. Really cute, too."

"Really?" Mom always teases me about using certain words too much. She passed Dad a plate of string beans.

Of course I was happy. Brenda is my friend. It just felt a little weird, that's all. But I was excited for her. Really excited.

"Oh, Norrie, I've got some news that should cheer you up," said Mom. "Aunt Caroline called me today and said that Steffie and Brad are coming home for a visit."

I perked up. "Re — Seriously?"

Mom nodded. "Then Steffie's going to stay here and help out at the shop while the Navy sends Brad to the Middle East for few weeks."

The shop belongs to my aunt Caroline, in Rehoboth, just across the state line in Delaware. She sells jewelry. Steffie's husband, Brad, is a naval officer.

"That sounds dangerous," said my father. "You never know what's going to happen next out there."

"Hmmm, but at least Steffie's getting out of Mississippi," said Mom. "Apparently she wasn't adjusting too well."

"She *hated* it," I interjected. "She said Mississippi was the worst place on Earth, and that the women there were really mean and jealous of her."

"Well, maybe she didn't give them much of a chance," Mom said. "Nobody ever said being a Navy wife would be easy."

"Trouble is, she thought it would be all receptions and balls, like at the Academy," said Dad, shaking his head. "Unrealistic expectations, married much too young — "

"After only one year of college," added Mom. "Poor Caroline! That nearly broke her heart."

They looked at each other and then they looked at me. My parents would absolutely *die* if I didn't go to college. I wasn't even sure you needed to go to college to be a photojournalist, but I didn't say anything. I'm not stupid.

"Don't you get any crazy ideas about marrying that young," warned my dad. "Get yourself an education first, or else you'll wind up screwing up your life like your cousin."

"How can you say that?" I demanded indignantly. "Steffie really loves Brad! You should hear what she went through to get him! And he's absolutely nuts about her! Remember the wedding last year?"

Steffie and Brad had gotten married at the Academy. It was so beautiful and romantic. Traditional, too, with the bride and groom coming out of the church and walking underneath a canopy of swords held up by Brad's friends. Really, the whole thing was like something out of a storybook, and Steff had chosen me as one of her bridesmaids.

"Who could forget that extravaganza?" said my father. "The reception in the fanciest hotel in Annapolis, a six-piece band, gardenias in the pool, and white doves flying all over the goddamned place. What Caroline and her ex spent on that wedding could have sent three kids to college." He glared at me. "That bridesmaid's dress cost us one hundred and twenty bucks, and now it just sits in the closet. Where you're going to wear it again, I have no idea."

I stayed silent on that point. I could have mentioned a prom, but, actually, I didn't like the dress all that much. It was too frilly and too pastelly, and I was hoping he'd forget about it before I actually got invited to a prom.

"It was the best wedding ever!" I told him. "Like a royal wedding — wasn't it, Mom?"

"Yes, it was," she agreed. "But I'm not sure it was worth it. Norrie, help me clear up so we can get out of here, will you? And don't look at me like that, honey. I'm just worried your cousin might be heading for a fall."

"I don't know," muttered Dad to his plate. "It might do her some good."

Four

It was during the last part of June when summer arrived with a vengeance. It was hot, unbearably hot, the kind of hot that dries the sweat right on your skin, but leaves slushy places under your arms and in the crooks of your elbows. The tourists seemed to be spending more time in the water than on the beach, and I seemed to be spending most of my paycheck on cool drinks and zinc oxide.

I was working nearly every day, out in the sweltering sun, staggering like a drunk under the weight of my Nikon. It never used to be so heavy, but I never used to have to carry it around my neck for eight hours at a time. Plus, I was developing muscles in all the wrong places. Already I had the neck and shoulders of an NFL linebacker. By the end of summer, I knew I'd be able to qualify for a position on the Russian women's shot-put team.

The one thing that wasn't hot was my love life. That was so frigid, I kept expecting some explorer to come by and plant a flag in me. Like the North Pole, get it? *Nothing* was happening. Mark was nice and friendly to me, it's true, but more like a buddy. God, I didn't see how things could possibly get worse.

Oh, yeah, one thing did make it worse: Brenda was now officially deliriously in love, and it was getting kind of hard to take. I mean, of course I was glad that she was so happy, and that they were so good together, but she talked about Peter *endlessly.* I hardly ever got a chance to get a word in about Mark anymore.

One day we were having lunch together, as usual enjoying the air-conditioning and avoiding the fries, and I asked her if she thought I should dye my hair blonde.

"I could use that Sun-In stuff, so it wouldn't be so obvious," I told her. "Or maybe I should just go all the way with some Miss Clairol. I don't know, I wouldn't want to screw up my hair forever. What do you think?"

"Are you out of your mind?" she gasped. "Don't you *dare*! It always looks so tacky. Peter says . . ."

I sighed and tuned out the rest of Peter's wisdom. I liked the guy a lot, but I wasn't going to take hair coloring advice from him, for God's sake.

". . . Why don't you just be yourself?" she finished.

"Being myself hasn't done anything for me so far. Have you ever noticed how fewer blond boys there are than blonde girls? What does that tell you?"

"Just because a lot of girls do it, doesn't make it any less tacky," she replied, sounding, I thought, too much like a mother.

I fingered my bangs. "Don't you think I've picked up some blonde highlights from being in the sun so much?"

"Hmmm," she murmured noncommittally. She was right. Highlights or no, my hair was still basically brown.

"What's wrong with brown hair, anyway?" I demanded aggressively. "Venus had brown hair, and she was the goddess of love! A lot of history's most beautiful women have had brown hair. Mark has brown hair, and I don't hold it against him! I *like* brown hair!"

"So do I," said Brenda. "And so does Peter, especially with light eyes. Peter says . . ."

Blah, blah, blah.

". . . Maybe we could fix you up with one of Peter's friends."

I ignored that last part, just as I had ignored the first. I had already told Brenda that I did not want any charity dates. It was Mark or nothing.

Brenda must have noticed my silence, because she changed the subject. I was half listening to her talk about how much she hated fries, and how the heat of the stand was turning her into a complete frizz-ball, but Peter still liked her hair, and wasn't he *so* sweet, when someone sat down on the stool next to me. I automatically moved my camera toward our side of the counter and continued listening to Brenda.

"Nice camera," a voice commented, and I gave him a quick look. College age. Light brown hair that strag-

43

gled around his neck and ears. Not bad-looking, if you like the type. My eye caught the glimmer of a gold earring dangling from his ear.

"We match," he said, smiling, then he reached up and pushed my hair aside to compare our gold hoops. I immediately pulled away. I don't like people touching me when I don't even know them. "Sorry, I didn't mean to scare you."

"You didn't scare me," I said stiffly and moved closer to Brenda.

"Ohh — you got her pissed off now," said the guy's friend, laughing like it was some kind of huge joke.

"Let's get out of here," whispered Brenda, and I nodded, starting to get my stuff together. Then I saw Mark walking in with an older blonde girl in tow. Only if she was blonde, I was the Queen of England — her hair color had that brassy look that said it came right out of a bottle. Mark didn't seem to think that was tacky.

"On second thought, I think I'll stay here and finish my drink," I told her, sitting back down on my stool. Brenda looked at me like I was crazy, but I pretended not to notice. I knew she wasn't about to say something in front of these guys.

"If that's what you want," she said coolly. "I'll catch up with you *later*." Earring and his friend turned as she walked past, but Brenda didn't even glance at them.

The one sitting next to Earring hooted, "Hey, your friend doesn't seem too friendly."

"She's shy," I told him.

"Shy? Come on, girl, don't be shy — hey, where are you running off to?" he yelled to her back. Brenda ignored him, but he had accomplished one thing —

he had gotten Mark's attention. And Mark had recognized me, sitting with two older guys.

"Your friend sure was in a hurry," Earring said. "I was hoping the four of us could talk some."

"She doesn't talk much," I explained. "She's got a boyfriend."

"How about you?"

"How about me what?" I countered.

Earring smiled. "Are you shy, too?"

I shrugged. "Sometimes."

He smiled again, nodding his head while he looked me up and down. It made me really uncomfortable, and I wished I had gone with Brenda. But then I remembered Mark.

"My name's Rick," Earring said. "This is Jim," he added, jerking his head in the other guy's direction.

"I'm Norrie."

"That's a pretty name," said Rick, which is about as humongous a lie as you can get. "Where are you from, Norrie?"

"Nearby. And you guys?"

"Baltimore," Rick answered. "We heard it was ten degrees cooler here on the beach than in the city. Took the weekend off for the waves."

"Fun in the sun," Jim leered, leaning over the counter. "You like to have fun, Lori?"

"Her name is Norrie." Rick shoved him. "Don't you have someplace else to be?" he demanded, and the next minute Jim was melting away like the Wicked Witch of the West or something. Talk about obvious! Rick looked back at me and smiled. "Are you still in high school?"

"Y-es." Out of the corner of my eye, I saw that Mark

was glancing our way. I leaned my arms on the counter, closer to Rick, and forced myself to smile. "I'll be a senior soon." It wasn't really a lie; two years is fairly soon. Time flies, doesn't it?

"Senior year's the best," Rick said. "I'll be a sophomore at Towson State this year."

"That's nice," I mumbled, watching Mark and the blonde leave with their drinks. I started gathering up my stuff. "Well, time to get back to work," I said cheerfully. "See you around."

"Hey, what's the rush?" he asked. "Why don't we get together later?"

"Gee, I'm really busy with work and all — "

"What's your number? I'll call you."

"Oh, I'm never home. Give me yours," I suggested. "I'll call you."

"Sure," he said, but I could tell that he knew I had no intention of calling him. Still, he was a good loser, writing it down on a scrap of paper anyway. I barely gave him enough time to finish before I was walking away.

I didn't see Mark again until later that evening at the studio. He was showing me how to develop color photographs, which is a lot different and a lot harder than black and white. He was practicing on some of his own shots, so it wasn't really that big a deal for him.

I'd asked him to show me how to do it several weeks ago. Another one of my bright ideas. I figured we'd be in a darkroom, I mean, a real *dark* room, right? Alone in a *darkroom*. Sharing our great mutual love of photography while alone in a darkroom. Surely one thing would lead to another. I didn't see how I could possibly miss.

But, as usual, Mark was acting perfectly normal — which is to say, all business. He didn't even mention seeing me with Rick. He just talked about developers and fixers until I thought I'd like to fix *him* with a right hook to the jaw. Yes, I still loved him, but it would have given me such pleasure just to really slug him one.

"So, how's the dating service going?" he asked. This was his new joke. Seeing me talking to lots of different boys hadn't done anything but amuse him. He teased me by saying I only took this job to improve my love life.

"How's yours?" I retaliated. In the dim red light I could see the grin on his face. The stinker.

"Why? You want to compare notes?"

"No, my mother doesn't let me read those kinds of books," I said sweetly. "She worries a lot about corrupting influences."

"So your mother worries a lot about you?"

I shrugged. "No more than any other. How about yours?"

"Well, it's hardly the same, you know." He took the last of the prints out and handed them to me to hang up. They were mostly candid shots of tourists doing funny things, like the close-up of the little kid with his face smeared with cotton candy, and the one of a man taken just as he's waking up after falling asleep in the sun, and suddenly realizing he's sunburned everywhere except for where his hands were resting on his stomach. I think that one was my favorite, but they were all really excellent.

I stood admiring them, thinking I'd never have Mark's eye for catching the absolutely right moment, when he said, "I'm wondering if you aren't getting in over your head."

"How so?" I asked, startled. I didn't think I'd done so badly with the color developing. Was I doomed to black and white forever?

Mark opened his mouth to speak, and then shook his head. "Nothing. Never mind."

I watched him putting the print paper away, knowing there was more. "Look," he said finally, "it's none of my business, but I just think a kid like you should maybe try sticking to guys her own age."

This was so different from what I'd expected that for a second, I wasn't sure I'd heard right. Then I said fiercely, "I am *not* a kid! I'll be sixteen in a few months!" (Nine months, but who's counting?) "You're only two years older than me, and girls mature a lot faster than boys, so that means you're the one who's just a kid here," I added.

"Okay, okay, have it your way, you're not a kid," he conceded. "Jeez, forget I ever mentioned it."

Right then it occurred to me that I wasn't playing this right. I had been so infuriated by the word "kid" that I had let the fact that he was — might be — *jealous* slip right by me. Now I felt myself go all gooey inside.

"What's the matter?" I said softly. "Don't you think I can take care of myself?"

He shook his head and turned on the light. "I think you're a brat, that's what I think."

And, then, before I could tell him that he was a bigger brat than I ever *thought* about being, he walked out. So there I was, alone in the darkroom, biting my lip in frustration and looking around for something to break. Preferably with Mark's head.

Two minutes later he stuck that head back in. "I almost forgot to ask you something."

"*What?*" I snapped.

"You doing anything for the Fourth?"

My heart took an immediate nosedive. "No," I said slowly, holding my breath. "Well, you know, nothing important."

"Like to go to a party?"

I was so floored, I thought for one moment that I was going to pass out. I swear, my heart actually stopped beating. "Wh — sure!" I said, tripping over the words. "Th-that sounds like fun," I added more calmly. No reason he had to know that I'd only been waiting for this moment my entire life.

"Great! It's at the condo of this girl I know; her parents are letting her use it for the weekend. It's got a balcony with a great view of the beach. She asked me to invite some friends. Bring a date if you want. You got somebody, or should we fix you up?"

I stared at him, confused, dumbfounded, not realizing at first what he was asking. Then it hit me. "Oh, sure," I said numbly. "I'll manage."

"That's what I thought," he said, grinning, but it was hard to hear him over the sound of my heart breaking. Mark took a pen and wrote something down on a piece of paper. "Here's the address. The party starts at eight. Got it?"

"Uh — got it." I took the piece of paper in my hands and forced a cheerful smile. "Thanks."

"No big deal," he replied, casually stepping over all

the broken pieces of my heart. "Don't forget to lock up!"

It took me several minutes to recover, but when I did I was *mad*. I was so mad, I didn't stop and reconsider what I was doing, so mad, I didn't even wait till I got home; I called Rick from a pay phone. It cost me two quarters because I had to wait a long time before he got to the phone. There seemed to be a lot of noise and confusion going on in his room.

"Hey, this is a surprise!" he exclaimed when I told him why I was calling. "Sure, I can come. But I don't have any wheels. Can you pick me up?"

"You don't need to drive; it's just down the boardwalk from you. I'll meet you there, okay?"

"I don't know this town too well. I might get lost," he said. "Why don't you meet me at my hotel instead?"

Because I'm not stupid. "Oh, it's real easy," I told him. "You couldn't possibly get lost. I've got the address here — do you have something to write with?"

So he wrote it down and agreed to meet me there at eight. Score one more point for me.

Five

"Are you out of your mind?" Brenda yelled at me later that night. "That guy is bad news, Norrie. He's got one thing on his mind, and it isn't watching fireworks at a teenage party. You can't be that dumb — you must have seen what he's after."

"Well, he isn't going to get it, so what difference does it make? Come on, Bren, will you and Peter drive me to the party or won't you?"

"It makes a lot of difference," she insisted. "People see you hanging out with guys like that and pretty soon they start thinking all kinds of things."

I sighed and made a face at the telephone receiver. I didn't understand why, but ever since Brenda had started dating Peter, she'd become hopelessly old-fashioned.

"Lighten up, will you, please?" I demanded. "It's

51

only a party. What can happen at a party? You'll be there, Peter will be there, lots of other people will be there — "

"*Mark* will be there," she finished. "Norrie, I know what you're trying to do, and I just don't think it's a good idea. You never know, it might backfire on you."

"Don't worry, I know what I'm doing," I lied.

"God, I hope so."

"Just pick me up at about seven forty-five, please?"

"Fine," she muttered, resigning herself to the inevitable, I guess. "It's your life."

"Thanks, Bren," I said, glancing at my mom walking into the kitchen. "I've got to go now. Bye!"

"Did I hear you say you were going out?" Mom asked, looking at her watch. "It's a bit late, don't you think?"

"I was talking about tomorrow."

"Tomorrow?" Mom looked up from the glass of milk she was pouring. "But, honey, I thought you were going with us. We made plans to join the Robinsons on their boat."

"Sorry, Mom." I shrugged my shoulders helplessly. Not that I really wanted to watch my father and mother suck up to the boring old Robinsons, while I had to put up with their stuck-up, snotty little brat of a daughter on their incredibly huge and tacky boat, but Mom didn't need to know that. "I already made plans to go to a party with Brenda and her new boyfriend."

"Aren't you afraid you'll be a third wheel?"

"Oh, there'll be other kids from school there."

Mom nodded, putting some of the Mrs. Fields cookies she and Dad like on a plate. She and Dad have milk and cookies nearly every night. That's kind of cute, isn't it?

"Anyone I know?" she asked.

"Well, you know Brenda," I said. She didn't seem completely satisfied with that, so I added, "And Mark will be there, too."

"Oh, Mark," she said, smiling. "Well, then, I guess it's all right. I know he'll keep an eye on you."

"*Mother*," I groaned, "I don't need anyone to keep an eye on me."

"No, you're all grown-up now, aren't you?" She smiled again and brushed my hair away from my forehead. "I suppose your father and I will have to get used to the fact that our little girl doesn't want to spend all her time with the old folks anymore."

The old folks I don't mind so much; it's Mr. Robinson I can't stand. "Maybe next year, Mom," I told her. "We could go watch the fireworks from the beach, like when I was little."

"Oh, it's too crowded then. You can't even find a place to sit down," she complained. "Okay, honey, you have a good time, just don't come home too late, and be careful."

"Barbara," my father yelled from the den. "Hurry up, the movie's starting."

I got this kind of sad feeling as I watched my mother carry the tray into the den. There was a time when she made milk and cookies for the three of us. But I was little then. I'd outgrown that long ago. Except now I had a sudden intense craving for them. I poured myself a glass of milk and went into the den to mooch a few cookies.

I wished I could talk to Mom about Mark. But there was no way she would understand. She's from a different time, different generation. And she would kill me if she knew what I was really doing, planning to go out with someone as old as Rick. *No way* would she understand that. But time was running out for me. I just had to get Mark. I just *had to.*

I was really nervous about the party, and Brenda shooting me dagger looks of disapproval the whole ride over made it ten times worse. Rick was waiting for me as planned, thank God, but I got even more nervous when I saw him. He was so much taller and bigger than I'd remembered, I guess because I'd only seen him sitting down.

"Hey, babe, you look outrageous," he said, kind of gawking at the neckline of my shirt. This was a bad start; I really detest being called "babe." It's so impersonal, like the guy can't even remember what your name is. I don't much like "Norrie," either, but at least it's mine. And what did he mean, "outrageous"?

I was really regretting the whole thing until we walked into the party. The look on Mark's face when he saw me with Rick made it all worthwhile.

Mark introduced us to Karen, who was the same girl I'd seen him with the other day. The cradle-snatching blonde! She was all smiles, telling us how glad she was we could come, but I figured it was an act. I hoped it was an act; I really didn't want to have to like her.

"Thanks for inviting us," I said, even though I knew she hadn't, really.

"Thanks for coming." Karen beamed. "Please help

yourselves to food and drinks — the table's by the stereo."

She pointed in the direction of the table, but there were already so many people crowded into the room, you couldn't see it. "You stay here, I'll get it," said Rick. "What do you want?"

"A Coke."

He came back a few minutes later, but whatever he gave me sure wasn't just Coke. I took one sip and nearly spit it out.

"What is this?"

"Haven't you ever heard of rum and Coke? Go on, drink it up and relax. It'll help get the party going."

He put his arm around me, but I moved away quickly so that he had to let go. I didn't want him touching me. I didn't want to drink rum and Coke, either, since I really don't like the taste of liquor. The few times I've been in this situation before, I've always managed to dump out the drink. But there were no plants in the room, and the kitchen might as well have been miles away. So I started sipping it. My hands needed something to do, anyway, and I sure as heck did need to relax.

"Want to dance?" he asked, and I nodded. Physical activity is always a good idea in situations like these. I took a big gulp of my drink and let him take my hand. He didn't let go of it, even though the music was fast, and when a slow song came on, he was way too quick to pull me into his arms.

"Great party!" I said, trying to keep some distance between us. "Lots of people here."

"They seem a little young to really party hardy."

Rick eyed the crowd critically. "How old did you say you are?"

"I'll be eighteen in a few months," I lied. It wasn't technically a lie; thirty-two months is a few months for some people. For someone really old, it isn't any time at all. It has to do with relativity, you know.

"Just seventeen, if you know what I mean?" Rick asked, giving me that look again. I didn't know what he meant, but I had an idea it wasn't good. But my head was getting fuzzy, and it was hard to think properly.

"Whew, I'm thirsty," said Rick, dragging me over to the table. Everybody knows you should never drink on an empty stomach, and I hadn't eaten much at dinner, so I tried to grab some potato chips as we went past. Rick put another drink in my hand.

"I think I'd rather have just plain Coke," I told him.

"They ran out. Relax, it's only Lite beer."

I figured that meant less alcohol, so I started to drink it. It tasted better than the rum and Coke, and easier to get down. I tried another swipe at the chips, but the fireworks were about to start, so we all drifted onto the balcony.

The fireworks display is one of the reasons the Fourth of July is so superb in Ocean City. They really do a spectacular job. They shoot them off from the beach so that they explode over the water. It's so dark over there that the fireworks really light up the sky. I love it.

But this year I wasn't enjoying it so much. First, I was feeling kind of dizzy. Second, Rick had his arm around me and his hand kept stroking my arm until I thought I would scream at him to *take it away*. I decided to let it stay there when I saw Mark with his arm around Karen.

Naturally, I pretended to enjoy the show. I oohed and aahed and clapped at all the right times. But I wasn't paying attention to the fireworks; I was looking at Mark and Karen.

Suddenly I found myself thinking of how I could slip Weight-On tablets into her drink without anyone noticing. I wondered how long those things take to work. It would be truly ideal if she'd bloat up from a size six to sixteen in one evening, but I knew it had to take longer than that.

Then I pictured myself sneaking into the bathroom and putting something in her shampoo. Green food coloring. Bug spray. Something really gross like that. Maybe she'd even have to cut all her hair off. Yeah, and then her hair would grow back to its real color, and Mark would see her for the phony she really is.

Of course, I'd feel really bad if somebody else used her shampoo, somebody I didn't even know, and ended up with green hair. That would be just awful.

Mark leaned closer to Karen and said something in her ear. She laughed. Suddenly the things I was thinking in my head turned downright ugly. I pictured the two of us swimming, and me pushing her in the way of a blonde-eating shark that would tear her limb from pretty limb so that even her own mother wouldn't recognize her.

Whoa, this was getting out of hand. The jealousy I was feeling was so strong that it was starting to scare me. I turned quickly away from the sight of Mark nuzzling her ear, and drew a sharp breath.

"Have another beer," Rick whispered, and I took the cup from his hand. I drank it fast, much faster than you should.

"All right!" Rick said, chuckling. "Just like a pro. Feeling happy yet?"

I flashed him one of my best smiles. "Getting there," I agreed. It was true; I was starting to feel giggly and lighthearted, and that was just fine by me.

The big finale came: red, white, and blue everywhere and lots of noise. You could barely hear the music they were playing over all the noise. Everybody started hooting and clapping.

"Outrageous!" said Rick, and then we all drifted back inside.

We danced some more and drank some more, and I discovered I kind of like beer — even if it does make you have to go to the bathroom a lot.

Brenda caught my arm just as I was coming out of there for the third time. "Norrie," she whispered. "I think you'd better cool it."

"Cool it? Too hot to cool it," I told her, laughing.

She gave me a stern look, barely glancing at Rick. "Peter and I are leaving now, if you still want a ride with us."

I grabbed at Peter's wrist, trying to reach for his watch, and stomped on his foot instead.

"Sorry," I giggled. "If you would just stand still so I could read this thing."

Peter sighed and held his watch up to my face.

"Aw, come on, it's early yet, why you wanna leave?" I exclaimed, poking at his hand.

"It's past eleven," Peter said.

"Past your bedtime, huh?" I asked, waving them away. "You two old fogeys go ahead. I'll get a ride home with somebody else."

Brenda and Peter exchanged looks.

"Don't worry. I'll be okay," I told them, leaning on Rick for support. "Ricky'll take care of me, won't you, babe?"

Brenda gave me this fed-up look, and then they stalked out, but I was having such a good time, I barely noticed. Rick had challenged me to a chugging contest: That's where you have to drink the whole glass of beer in one swallow, without stopping, with everybody around cheering you on.

I won.

Mark tried to get me aside. "Norrie, I think you've had enough," he muttered, but I wasn't in the mood to listen.

"Who cares what you think?" I told him, and wobbled toward Rick. He handed me a beer, and I downed it in one gulp, looking straight at Mark. He gave me a disgusted look and went back to Karen.

After that, I decided I was going to get *really* happy. I was laughing and telling jokes — I never knew I could be so funny! And then we danced some more, and I was moving it like I was a dancer on MTV, you know? I never knew drinking could make you dance so much better.

But it was stuffy in the room, in spite of the a.c., and I was sweating when Rick pulled me against him to dance slow. "It's hot," I complained, lifting the hair off of my neck. "I need another drink."

"I've got a better idea," he said, and then he put

some ice down my blouse. I screamed and tried to get him back, but he was too fast for me. By then I was laughing so hard, my head was spinning around and around like a top, and I couldn't seem to stand up straight.

"I know where it's cool," Rick said, pulling me out of the room. He led me down the hallway and the next thing I knew, we were in a room, and he had closed the door behind us.

There was a big fan blowing on the dresser. I swayed for a few moments before I managed to stagger over and stand in front of it.

"That does feel better," I said appreciatively, letting the wind blow over my hot face and neck. "But we shouldn't be in here — "

"Shh, relax," he said, his arms coming up from behind. "No one's going to bother us."

I felt his lips on my neck, and then his hands were all over me. I wanted to push him away, but my head was reeling so much that I had to hold on to him instead, otherwise I would have fallen.

"Please stop, Rick," I said as firmly as I could. "I think we should go back to the party."

He was in front of me now, pushing me toward the bed. "Come on, babe," he whispered, his hands on my blouse. I tried to pry them away, but I wasn't as strong as I thought I was. Or maybe it was that he was so much stronger. Or maybe it was the beer. I just couldn't get him off me.

"Relax, will you?" he muttered. I twisted my head, struggling, but he wouldn't stop.

"I said, *stop it*, Rick! I mean it!" But he didn't seem

to hear me. I was scared, really scared, wondering if I would have to scream, wondering if anyone would hear over the noise of the party. . . .

"Let go of me," I warned, panting, "or I'll — "

Wham! The door suddenly burst open, and there stood Mark, glaring at us like an avenging angel.

Six

I felt like crying. From relief, from embarrassment, I don't know which. I just wanted to cry.

"Hey, man, what gives?" protested Rick. "This is a private party, you know?"

Mark looked at Rick like he was a slug, like something he'd step on, if it were worth the bother. "She's only fifteen."

"Say what?" Rick yelped, backing away from me, like being fifteen was a contagious disease. "She told me she was a senior!"

"She lied," said Mark.

I cringed, trying to inch my way off the bed. "Why, you little b — " Rick began threateningly, but Mark cut him off.

" —Just get lost," he advised. "Unless you want trouble."

"Me?" Rick snorted in disgust, spreading his hands in front of him. "Hey, no sweat. I'm gone. You don't catch me messing around with jail bait. No way. Shit, you can keep her."

He was out of the room without even a backward glance. I made an effort to pull myself together, but I was so dizzy! Mark just grabbed me by the wrist and wrenched me up.

"Let's go," he muttered, his face so hard and angry that he frightened me almost as much as Rick had. He started to drag me behind him, and I stumbled.

"Ouch! You're hurting me!"

"Good!"

Karen was standing by the door, her mouth forming a little "o" of dismay. "Is she all right?" she asked.

"No," he replied grimly. "She's wasted. Very wasted."

"Oh! Well, I thought she was a little young to be drinking that much." Karen looked at me sympathetically. "Poor thing!"

"Yeah, poor thing," he agreed, glowering at me. "I'm sorry about this, Karen, but I've got to take the kid home. I'll call you tomorrow, okay? Norrie, apologize to Karen for being such an ass and spoiling her party."

"Oh, that's all right, she didn't spoil anything," said Karen quickly. "Just drive carefully, Mark."

I knew I was drunk, but I wasn't so gone I didn't see her turn the sympathetic look from me to him. Wonderful, nice Mark to help out the nasty little drunk kid. He gave her a look, too, one that said, "I'll be back as soon as I get rid of the ass." Then he dragged me down to the car.

Alone at last, I thought as he shoved me into the passenger side. He locked the door. Why did he lock the door? Did he think I was going to fall out? That struck me as so funny that I started to laugh, and then I couldn't stop. I kept laughing and laughing like it was the best joke I'd ever heard. Me falling out of his car. Norrie Plimmon, drunk and disorderly, body parts strewn all over Ocean Drive.

"Shut up," Mark hissed. "Or do you want me to slap you?"

That did stop me cold. Just as suddenly as I had started laughing, now I started to cry. "Do you have to be so mean?" I moaned. "I don't feel so good."

"You'll feel worse, *and* you deserve it," he replied. "You really are a jerk, do you now that? Didn't I tell you you were in over your head? But, no, you had to go prove to everybody how sophisticated and mature you are. Mature! I've got a three-year-old niece who's more mature than you are!"

"I'm sorry," I whimpered, wishing he would stop. My head was starting to clear, by my insides were churning around like a washing machine.

"Sorry?" he banged his fist against the dashboard and I jumped. "Do you have any idea what could have happened to you if Karen hadn't noticed you were gone? You sure know how to pick them! That slimeball was all over you! But, no, *you* can take care of yourself! Jesus, that's rich! Your parents should lock you up in the house until you grow some brains!" He paused. "Well?" he demanded. "Don't you have anything to say?"

"I think I'm going to throw up."

Mark muttered a very bad word and then pulled over to the side of the road. He reached over me to open the door and pushed my head down, holding me there while I emptied out what little there was in my stomach.

When it was all over, Mark handed me a Kleenex. "Feel better?" he asked, less angrily now.

I nodded, still the most miserable I have ever been in my life. Physically I felt better, but inside I just wanted to die, really *die*.

"I'm sorry," I mumbled. "I think I got some on your car."

"Don't worry about it."

"I've never been drunk before. It's awful."

"Now you know," he said. "Don't do it again."

"No, never," I promised. "It's just awful."

Mark didn't scream at me anymore on the way home. I guess he figured he'd given me enough hell for one evening. I turned my face to the window and looked out into the darkness through the blur of my tears. They were poised there, in the corners of my eyes, waiting to fall; one blink and I would have been a goner. I didn't blink, not once during the horrendous trip home. I was that desperate to keep from crying.

I knew I'd lost him for good this time. No guy was going to look romantically at a girl who lets herself get pawed by some creep and then throws up right in front of him, practically in his car. And all the things he'd said to me! I deserved every one of them. This time I'd blown it forever.

I didn't look at him when I got out of the car to go into my house. I thanked him and apologized, but I just couldn't look at him. I knew if I did I would lose control, and the tears would start to pour. I just had to make it to the house before doing that.

I'd shamed myself enough for one evening.

When I woke up early the next morning, my whole face hurt; my throat was sore, and I had a splitting headache. For one second I thought I had the flu.

And then I remembered.

I looked at the wall next to my bed, plastered with pictures of Mark. There was Mark at a Yearbook meeting, with his feet up on the desk, wearing those old Nikes I loved so much. There was Mark on the beach, talking to some kids. There was Mark walking toward me on the boardwalk, grinning, with the sun shining on his hair. There was Mark, lost to me forever.

All the plans and schemes and hopes, all the months, all the wishing — all for this. Nothing.

I didn't think I had any more tears left, but I did. This time I cried until they were all gone.

I finally got out of bed several hours later, dying of thirst. I went into the bathroom and took two aspirin with lots of water. My throat still ached, though, I guess from crying.

I caught my reflection in the mirror and groaned. I looked like an old hag. My eyes were red and swollen, and my whole face looked pasty and puffy. I washed it twice, once with cold water and once with warm, but it didn't look any better. No wonder Mark didn't love me, with a face like that, I thought. I looked ugly. I *was* ugly. How come I'd never noticed that before?

I took my hand and slammed it against the mirror. I wanted to hurt that face, the face that Mark couldn't — or wouldn't — love. Blam! I slammed it again, harder this time. Then I heard my mother outside the door.

"Norrie, are you finally up? Did you have a good time at the party?"

I gripped the sides of the sink and tried to sound normal. "It was okay."

She started telling me about their adventure on the Robinsons' boat. The fact that the door was closed didn't appear to faze her at all. I sighed and started brushing my teeth, listening as best I could.

It seemed the boat had run aground, and they'd had to wait until the tide changed before they could get off again, because Mr. Robinson refused to pay someone to come and help him. That's why they hadn't heard me come in — because they hadn't come home until after me. I said a silent thank-you to Mr. Robinson for being so cheap. He'd saved my butt for sure.

"Norrie?" Mom was still outside the door. "Are you all right, dear?"

I took a deep breath and opened the door. Mom looked at me and gasped. "You look terrible! What happened to you last night?"

"Nothing. I told you, it was okay. I came home early, though. I think maybe I got a flu bug or something."

"Do you want me to get you something?"

I shook my head. "Nah, I'm just going back to sleep. Thanks anyway, Mom."

She looked troubled, but didn't say anything. I gently closed the door on her and got back into bed.

• • •

Several hours later, there was another knock on the door. "Norrie?" I heard Brenda call. She knocked again and stuck her head in. "Norrie? Your mom said you were up here. Can I come in?"

"Sure," I mumbled. "But please stop making so much noise. I have a headache."

"Yeah, your mom said you weren't feeling well. It's a good thing she doesn't know it's a hangover." She looked disapprovingly at me, but then I guess pity and curiosity took over. "So what happened after Peter and I left?"

So I gave her the whole story, shortened version. My head was too cottony to do it all. Afterwards, she just shook her head and sighed.

"I'll never get him now," I finished miserably. "All my planning and scheming, all those months — all for nothing. I've lost him for good this time."

Brenda shook her head and sighed some more. She didn't even contradict me. That was a first.

"What were you trying to prove getting drunk like that?" she demanded. "That was just plain stupid."

"Oh, lighten up, Bren. If you and Peter can play tonsil hockey every time the lights go out, I can have a few drinks."

"Peter and I have a *relationship*," she said indignantly. "And he certainly wasn't all over me like that Rick guy was on you. Like white on rice."

I turned my face to the wall. If she started talking about Peter again, I was going to scream. She was an expert on love, after only a few weeks? I'd been hooked on Mark since last September — ten months, three days, five hours, and twenty minutes ago. Now *that* was true love.

Brenda must have seen my tears, because she suddenly stopped with the usual blah-blah about how wonderful Peter was, and sighed. "You have so much going for you, Norrie," she said suddenly. "Don't waste it on somebody who doesn't love you back. You need to find someone crazy about *you*."

I kept my face to the wall. "What can I do? I'll never love anyone the way I love Mark."

The next few days were awful, truly awful. My parents must have realized something was wrong, but they didn't say anything, thank God. My father looked at me strangely a couple of times, like he suspected I was on drugs or something. Jeez, you'd think he would know me better. I mean, I was a mess, but I wasn't completely screwed up.

The one good thing I had to look forward to was Steffie and Brad's visit. They came over for dinner with Aunt Caroline on their second night back.

"Norrie!" Steffie exclaimed, hugging me. "You're so skinny! What happened to all your baby fat?"

I'd lost five pounds in the last week or so, but I didn't tell her that. I just hugged her back, hard.

"You look fabulous!" I said, falling back into my old role as the admiring younger cousin. "As always!" I was so happy to see her that I felt like crying, if that makes any sense. Steffie always makes me feel better, but also a little sad.

Brad hugged me, too, which I thought was really nice of him. We'd only met the one time at his wedding, when I was one of the junior bridesmaids. He'd been so handsome and sophisticated that I'd been very shy and awkward around him. He still made me feel that way a little bit, although I know he didn't try to. He and Steff were both so fabulous, you couldn't help but be in awe of them.

Over dinner, they told us all about their plans.

"Thank goodness we escaped from Mississippi," said Steffie with feeling. "Aunt Barbara, you wouldn't believe how dreary it is there. And the people are so rednecky!" She made a face. "It was horrible!"

Mom glanced at Brad and asked quickly, "Can you tell us anything about what you'll be doing in Turkey, Brad?"

"Sweating, probably," he shrugged, cutting his steak. "I wish they'd send me to some place cool for a change."

"You can't believe how hot it is in Mississippi," said Steffie. "Brutal, just brutal."

"Well, it's pretty hot here, too, Steff," Brad said mildly.

"At least we have the breezes," Steffie replied stonily. "And the air-conditioning works! Honestly, one more day in that Mississippi heat, and I thought I'd slit my throat!"

There was a little silence. "It's not the heat, it's the humidity," Mom said weakly, but Steffie didn't hear her.

"You don't know how glad I am to be back on the East Coast," she said. "Back to where you can understand people when they talk. Back to where there are more important things to do then sit around and listen to a bunch of cows in polyester pants brag about their

70

screaming brats. And here there are decent restaurants and the theater and — "

" — the stores," Brad finished for her. "Come on, Steff, that's what you really miss."

"Well, excuse me that I hated having to shop at the base exchange. Their idea of high fashion is stuff from the Sears catalog. Even my mother wouldn't wear some of the crap they sell."

"Oh, I don't know, I'm not much for clothes," interjected Aunt Caroline mildly. Steffie ignored her.

Dad looked at Mom and cleared his throat. "Brad, how about some more rice?" he asked, practically throwing the bowl in his face. "So, tell us, how long will you be able to stay in Rehoboth?"

Rehoboth is where my aunt lives. Like Ocean City, it's also a resort town, but a lot smaller. It's just across the state line, in Delaware.

"I leave for Turkey next week," said Brad. "When I get back, I'll have to be in Washington for about a month."

"I'm going to stay all summer," said Steffie. "I'll be helping Mom in the shop, right, Mom?"

Aunt Caroline nodded, but she didn't look so thrilled. I was, and I told Steffie so.

"Thanks, cuz," she said. "It'll be great to see all my old friends, visit my old haunts. I've really missed everybody. It'll be like old times."

"Not too much like old times, I hope," said Aunt Caroline casually. "You're a married woman now, after all."

"Yes, *Mother*, I remember," replied Steffie, giving her a hard look. "When Brad gets back from Turkey, he'll come up to visit on weekends."

"Well, whenever I can get away," Brad reminded her. "It might not always be possible, honey."

Steffie tossed her hair. "Then don't come, if it's too much trouble."

Brad sighed. "I didn't mean it that way. We've been over this a thousand times — "

"Yes, I know, the Navy comes first."

"It's my job. You knew how it was when you married me."

"It's a wonder anyone can even get here from D.C.," Mom interrupted desperately. "The traffic coming over from the Western Shore gets worse every year. When are they going to finish widening the bridge, that's what I'd like to know."

"Won't matter, it still won't be wide enough," Dad said. "Too many bottlenecks. What we need is a free-way."

"Oh, no," said Aunt Caroline. "That would be terrible! In no time at all the Eastern Shore would look like the Jersey Turnpike. I'm all for doing something about the traffic, but we don't want to jeopardize the quality of life out here, do we?"

That started them in on the usual discussion about the pros and cons of continued expansion. My aunt is definitely against it, but, then, she really likes the quiet life, like you get in Rehoboth. She sells jewelry at her shop — off-beat, unique kinds of jewelry, some of it made from shells. Not tacky, but really nice stuff. She doesn't make a lot of profit, but she says she does all right. Steffie's father lives in Chicago. He used to send Aunt Caroline money for Steffie; he also used to send Steffie money to do whatever she wanted with it. I didn't know if he still did, now that she was married.

72

Brad and Steffie didn't say too much during the rest of the dinner. They didn't look at each other much, either, or touch each other. There was a kind of tension between them, but I figured it was due to the fact that they were about to be separated. I mean, I'd be tense, too, if Mark was going off on a dangerous mission to the Middle East. I probably wouldn't be arguing with him, though, like Steffie was doing.

But they sure did look great together. Really. The perfect couple.

Seven

I didn't get to talk to Steffie alone until the next day. We were stretched out on the beach by her mother's house, watching Brad going down to the water. We continued to watch him swim, even when all we could see was his sleek head bobbing in the waves and an occasional glimpse of muscular arms and well-defined shoulders.

I couldn't suppress a wistful sigh. "God, he is so gorgeous! I swear, Steff, you're about the luckiest person in the whole world."

She smiled, adjusting the bows on the top of her bright orange-and-pink bikini. Off to our right a couple of guys sitting on a miniscule hotel towel started to salivate. My fabulous cousin noticed, but she pretended not to. Steffie is very, very cool.

"What about you?" she asked. "How is it going with that guy?"

I shook my head. "Don't ask."

"Tell me," she urged, and so the whole miserable story came out. It took me fifteen minutes of nonstop talking, by the end of which I was sniffling into my Kleenex again, and Steffie was shaking her head.

"I see what the problem is," she said. "You were fighting fire with fire. What you need to do, Norrie, is fight fire with a nuclear bomb."

"I tried jealousy; it didn't work," I told her. "He doesn't care. He still thinks of me as a kid. I *am* a kid. A stupid, jerky little kid."

"Yes, well, you didn't handle that party so great," she admitted, which impressed me as the biggest understatement since Noah told his family to expect a little rain. "But I wouldn't give up hope completely, Norrie. If he didn't care at all, he wouldn't have gotten so ticked off at you."

"He got ticked off because, oh, I don't know, because he thought he was responsible for me. That's the kind of guy he is. *Responsible*. The Wally Cleaver–Richie Cunningham type."

Steffie wrinkled her nose. "Nothing personal, but he sounds like a real drag."

"Oh, no, he's perfect. He's the greatest guy, Steff. Well, outside of Brad, he's the greatest. He's the greatest *young* guy. You'd love him, trust me." I leaned back on the beach blanket and put my arm over my eyes to shield them from the sun. "What happened was all my fault. At least before, we were friendly. Now, he just sees me as a . . . a nuisance. Like a fly buzzing around his ears. Or a dog panting over his shoulder while he's driving his car. Or a cat in heat screaming under his window when he's trying to sleep. Or a — "

"Okay, okay, I get it," she interrupted, "but I still think you should give it time. Things might change." She rolled over to her side, almost losing her top in the process. The guys next to us grabbed their chests like they were having heart attacks.

As if I weren't demoralized enough. Sometimes having a glamorous older cousin can make you feel like leftover meatloaf.

Brad came running out of the water toward us, and every eye — every girl's eye, that is — swiveled toward him. Who could blame them? Brad in his itsy-bitsy European-style trunks, water sluicing down his incredibly golden body, is a sight mere words cannot adequately describe, trust me. Even I, as miserable and lovelorn as I was, couldn't help but appreciate the view.

"Water's great!" Brad said, panting, dripping wet on our blanket. He grinned and shook his head at Steff, spraying her with droplets of water.

"Brad, don't!" she shrieked. "I told you, I don't want to get wet!" She raked her fingers through her hair and eyed it critically.

"Now why go to the beach if you don't want to get wet?" he countered. "That's the stupidest thing I've ever heard."

"I don't want to have to wash my hair again before we go out tonight. What's so stupid about that?"

"Okay, okay, how about a walk on the beach?"

"Take Norrie." Steff rolled over onto her stomach. "I want to work on my tan some more."

"Any tanner and your skin might turn to leather. What about our tennis game later?"

"Norrie will play with you, won't you, Norrie? I need to do some shopping this afternoon."

Brad sighed and looked at me. "Right. Come on, Norrie, you're already starting to freckle. Let's leave the human lizard to it."

I got that feeling of being leftover meatloaf again. Or maybe cold mashed potatoes and flat Coke. But walking in sand is very good for your legs, and my tennis game definitely needed work. Besides, being seen with Brad was great for the ego and the reputation.

I just wished he wouldn't talk to me as if I were an Irish setter in need of exercise.

"Come on, Norrie, put some punch into it!" Brad shouted as yet another one of my volleys dribbled before the net. Wearily I positioned myself for one of his killer serves. As I had suspected, Brad totally outclassed me. We'd been playing for over an hour, and his hair was barely ruffled, while I was panting and wheezing all over the court. He didn't seem to mind, though.

"Good game!" he shouted after he creamed me for the third time. "You know, you're a lot better than Stephanie."

I could believe it. Steffie got her incredible figure the old-fashioned way: from nature. No aerobics, no sweating, no exercise for her. I've said it before, I'll say it again: Life is unfair.

Brad bounded over the net to where I was squatting on the ground, trying to catch my breath and rubbing my right knee.

"What's the matter?" he asked. "Did you hurt your-self diving for that last ball?"

I grimaced. "No, it just feels tight from the ankle on up."

"Here, let me look at it." He bent over and started feeling my calf. "Feels like it may be cramping up," he said matter-of-factly, massaging it. "How does that feel to you? Better?"

I nodded, turning redder, and it had nothing to do with the heat. Well, I couldn't help it. Brad would have that effect on any female, honest he would. It's just one of those laws-of-nature things.

"Tell you what," he suggested. "Tonight, when you get home, give it a good soak in a warm tub. That should do it."

"Okay. Thanks."

"Sure thing," he said, ruffling my hair, making me feel about seven years old. "Another game tomorrow?"

I groaned. "Why? So you can beat the tar out of me again?"

He laughed. "Tell you what, Norrie, we'll play every day until I have to leave. By then, you know, you'll be beating the tar out of me."

I groaned again, and let him help me up. Well, if I wasn't going to have any romance this summer, I guess I was going to need another outlet. At least tennis was a healthy one.

Brad still had his arm around me in his brotherly way as we walked back to the parking lot, past a group of senior girls from school. I could feel their curious eyes trained on my back as we got into his Alfa-Romeo. I could almost hear them saying "Huh! What's she got?" in their snooty, senior voices. Of course, they were turning puce with envy, and I wouldn't be human if I didn't admit it made me feel great.

I was at the photo store the next day when Mark walked in. He saw me and stopped. He looked like he'd like to go back out again, but knew he couldn't. Or maybe I was just being paranoid, because he smiled at me. Sort of an awkward smile, but it was still a smile.

"Hey, what are you doing here?"

"I work here, remember?" I still had a job, didn't I? At least I had before the party. Maybe after having to rescue me from some goon and throwing up in his car, Mark had changed his mind.

"Sure, I remember," he replied, his eyes shifting away for a second. "Long time no see. You okay?"

"I'm fine," I said as casually as I could. Of course, I knew what he was *really* asking. *Staying out of trouble? Gone on any more drunken binges?*

"How about you?" I asked.

"Busy, you know how it is."

As conversations go, this one wasn't exactly thrilling. I felt so tense that I was actually glad when Joe walked in from the back.

"Here are your pictures, Norrie," he said. "Looks like they came out good."

He handed me some family photos I'd taken. The top one was of Brad at the beach. I caught Mark's eye and nervously put them in my purse. He was looking distinctly pissed.

"I hope that's your own film you're using," he said. He'd said the exact same thing to me not so long ago, but in an entirely different way.

"Of course."

"You're not supposed to be using the store for your personal use," he added.

"I checked it out with Joe first." Joe had moved away, but he nodded from behind the cash register.

"As long as she doesn't make a habit out of it," Joe said, smiling. That was sort of a running joke between us.

"See that you don't," said Mark stiffly, looking at his watch. "Isn't it time you got to work?"

I nodded, so hurt by his tone that I could feel my eyes smarting with sudden tears. I thanked Joe and turned around, immediately bumping my knee into the steel frame of the door. It was painful, but I barely noticed, I was in such a hurry to get out of there.

Damn him, anyway! Why are boys so mean?

I was working over in my territory the next day when I suddenly spotted Mark, carefully stepping over suntanned bodies, his camera in hand. He looked up, and I realized he was coming to see me. I was petrified with fear. There could only be one reason Mark would want to see me.

"Hey, Norrie," he greeted me. "Can you spare a minute? I want to talk to you about something."

So I was getting the ax, I thought, sitting down next to him on the sand. Oh, jeez, couldn't he just have told me over the phone? Wouldn't that have been kinder?

I waited for him to begin. "How's business today?" he finally asked.

"Really good," I chirped. "I think this might be one

of my best days yet. I ran into a family with four little girls and two sets of grandparents, can you believe it? All together at once?"

"Hmmm, that was lucky," he agreed, but I could tell he wasn't really listening. He was scooping up handfuls of sand and letting it slide through his fingers. Slowly, purposefully, with *finesse*. I watched those long, well-shaped fingers with the clean, unbitten nails. I watched the sand. I wished *I* were the sand. Is that mental or what? Here I was, about to be fired, and I was still mesmerized by Mark. I swear, he can even make something as simple as picking up sand look unbelievably sexy.

It seemed forever until he spoke again. "I promised myself I wouldn't get involved," he said. "This is none of my business, but" — He paused and lowered his voice — "I thought you learned your lesson the other night at that party."

This was so different from what I'd been expecting that for a minute, all I could do was stare at him. "I don't know what you've been hearing," I said heatedly. "But I haven't had anything else to drink since then, I swear. I told you, never again!"

"I didn't mean that. I'm talking about that guy you've been seeing."

"What guy?"

"Okay, that *man*. The one in the photo. The one with the Alfa-Romeo and the terrific backhand."

I stared blankly at him. "You mean Brad?"

"Whatever. Remember we talked about being in over your head. Have you forgotten about that other creep?"

"No, but — "

"How old is he?" Mark demanded. "Does he know how old you are?"

"Of course, he does."

"Christ, he must be a real sicko."

"Now, wait a minute — "

"You are so naive, Norrie. You just don't know the first thing about anything, do you? Look, girl, the other night, at the party — "

"Yes, I know," I cut in. "I was an ass. You already told me. Are you going to keep throwing that in my face forever? I'm not a kid, you know, and you're not my father!"

"Yeah, and I'm plenty grateful, believe me!"

"Me, too!" I stared ahead to where two kids were building a sandcastle. Well, well! This was a strange turn of events, but something inside me wouldn't let me tell him who Brad really was. Could it be possible that Mark was jealous, after all?

"So why," I asked in a very calm voice, "are you so interested, anyway?"

That got him. He got this funny look on his face like he wanted to explode, but knew he had to keep his cool.

Eight

"And then he said, 'Oh, hell, go ahead, screw up your life, why should I care?', just like that," I was telling Steffie a little while later at my aunt's house. "What do you make of that? Do you think he could be jealous?"

Steffie was crowing with laughter. "Sure. What else? Wait till I tell Brad about this. He'll die!" And then she was laughing some more.

I shook my head disbelievingly. A bunch of senior girls was one thing, but how could Mark think that someone like Brad would actually go out with someone like me? "But that's ridiculous!" I said.

She shrugged. "Yeah, well, nobody said Mark was a rocket scientist. But this is super, Norrie. He played right into your hands, and you weren't even trying."

I didn't like the way she phrased that. It made me

vaguely uncomfortable. "I'd better tell him the truth next time I see him."

"Why would you do that?"

"Why? Because Brad is your husband!"

"No kidding," she countered, making her *I Love Lucy* face at me. "But if I don't mind, why should you?" She studied herself in the full-length mirror of her old room. She and Brad were going out to dinner, and Steff was dressed *to spill*. Her dress was so tight she could barely walk, but did she ever look superb. God, what a body. The kind you'd sell your grandmother's soul for.

In the mirror she caught my eye. "Listen, Norrie," she said, turning. "You have to decide. Do you want Mark, or don't you?"

I thought I'd given up on Mark, but now that Steff was asking me point-blank, I knew I'd been lying to myself. "Yes," I admitted. "I want him desperately. More than anything."

"Well, there you go. And Brad really made him sit up and take notice, didn't he? Isn't that what you want?"

"Yeah, Steff, but if he really thought that Brad was interested in me, wouldn't that scare him off? I mean, if I were a guy and I saw that Brad was my competition, I'd just say 'no contest' and quit."

"But you're not a guy. They like the challenge, believe me, and they all think they're totally irresistible. Look, I'm not saying you should lie to him, but there's no reason to make a big confession scene, either. Just be cool. And for Chrissake, don't tell him the truth!"

· · · ·

"You'd better tell him the truth," Bren told me very earnestly some time later at her house. "Honesty is the most important thing in a relationship. Peter says — "

"I'm not really interested in what Peter says," I interrupted. "I asked for *your* opinion. You can still think for yourself, can't you?"

I hadn't meant for it to come out like that, and of course Brenda got all defensive on me. "I most certainly do think for myself," she said coldly, "but in this case, I think Peter is right."

I sighed. "Of course. He always is."

Brenda ignored that. "Honesty is *extremely* important in a *mature* relationship. *Mature* people shouldn't have to play games with each other. You should have left that kind of stuff back in junior high."

Well, tie me up and force-feed me snail eggs until I spew, I thought. All this talk about maturity, and I was five months older than she was.

"He'll find out sooner or later, anyway," she added. "What if you and Mark actually do get serious? How are you planning to keep him from meeting Brad? You'd have to introduce them eventually."

"I'll worry about that when we announce our engagement," I said sarcastically. "Which isn't likely to happen, the way things are going."

"You're telling me. It'd be a miracle."

"What's that supposed to mean?"

She got up from the bed and went over to her desk. "Now don't get mad," she said, rummaging through some papers. "I cut out this article for you." She handed it to me. "Go ahead," she invited. "Read it. And don't get mad. I'm giving it to you for *your own good.*"

Ugh. Three words I absolutely detest. And the fact that she had asked me twice not to get mad, when I was already halfway there, made me sure that whatever was in this article, I was going to hate it.

And I was right. It was from one of those teen magazines, titled "Knowing When to Let Go." It was all about being in love with someone who doesn't love you, and how unrequited love isn't really love at all, and how destructive crushes can be.

Crushes? Did Brenda actually think that the deep, passionate feelings I had for Mark were anything even *close* to resembling a silly crush? This from my best friend, the girl who knew me better than anyone? We were so close, we each got our first period in the same week. How could she do this to me?

I wasn't so much angry, as really, really hurt. Brenda was anxiously looking at me.

"I just think it's time you moved on, Norrie," she said. "I mean, Mark isn't the only guy in the universe. I talked it over with Peter, and he knows some guys — "

"You did what?"

"Not everything," she said quickly, "just the basic facts, you know."

"Oh, no," I groaned. "You're joking, aren't you? Please tell me you're joking."

Brenda looked back at me defensively. "I just told him how concerned I was and everything, which was a good thing, because he suggested this friend of his — "

"I don't believe you!" *Now* I was angry. "You actually talked about my personal life with *Peter?*"

"Well," she mumbled, "a little bit. He is my boyfriend, Norrie."

"So what? Does that mean he gets to hear everything I shared with you *in confidence?*"

"It's really not that big a deal, Norrie. I just thought it might help to get a guy's opinion. Peter says — "

"For the last time, I am not interested in what Peter says. As a matter of fact, I am sick and tired of hearing Peter, Peter, Peter! Peter this and Peter that, every sentence out of your lousy mouth begins with Peter!"

Brenda opened her mouth, but I cut her off. "And another thing," I added. "I'm sick and tired of you always lording it over me, like what a *perfect* relationship you and Peter have. You've been going out for what? A couple of weeks, and suddenly you're this big-time authority on love and *relationships?* Well, let me tell you something, dear Ann Landers, you don't know diddly about real love, and you don't know diddly about guys, either!"

"Just because you're jealous doesn't mean you have the right to take it out on me," she retorted smugly.

"Jealous? Are you nuts? Jealous of you and *Peter?* If I wanted someone like Peter, I could get him, believe me."

"Oh, really? Then how come you don't?"

I glared at her. I don't think I've ever hated someone so much in my life. I ought to take Peter away from her, just to show her. But I wasn't sure I could.

"I'm getting the hell out of here," I told her.

"Fine with me," she snapped back. "Good-bye!"

"Good-bye!" I slammed her door behind me. I passed her father on the way out and almost knocked him over. He looked at me in surprise, holding on to his bowl of ice cream for dear life. I didn't answer his greeting, just ran out of their house and back to my own.

I was crying, and I was still so angry that colored lights were flashing around in my head. I felt like kicking something really hard. I tried thinking of ways to get back at her, but I couldn't think of anything beyond never speaking to her again. That didn't seem bad enough, somehow.

And behind it all, a voice in my head kept repeating, "She was my best friend. I've just lost my best friend."

I tried to put my fight with Brenda out of my head. Work kept me real busy, and now that Steph was spending so much time with her old schoolfriends, I was drafted to play tennis with Brad almost every day. On days we weren't playing tennis, he'd drag me to the beach for a swimming and running workout. I felt like I was being trained for the triathlon.

I saw Mark a few times when I was with Brad, but he never brought it up again, and I'd be darned if I was going to. Mark was acting so normal (translation: like he couldn't care less) that I began to think I'd imagined he might be jealous of Brad.

And then I had to ask him for Sunday off. You'd have thought I'd asked him for twenty years off his life.

"That's our busiest day," he complained for the third time. "Just because you've got a party going Saturday night doesn't mean you need a whole day off to recuperate."

"What party?" I asked, confused.

"The one your friend Brenda is having." He looked at me more closely. "Oh, that's too tame for you now, right? You and the Alfa-Romeo guy have something better planned?"

Brenda having a party! Obviously just so she could pointedly not invite me. That really hurt. But I managed to smile.

"Brad finds some of my friends a bit immature," I said, remembering what Brenda had told me last week. "He'd be terribly bored at a high school party." Well, that much was true, even if I had put my own spin on it, so to speak.

"Oh, would he?" I swear, Mark was almost *sneering*. "Would you think I was immature if I went?"

"*You're* going?"

"Well, I was invited." He smiled. "Now that I know I won't be watching out for you, I guess it's safe to go."

Was that a joke, I wondered? I didn't think it was very funny. How could Brenda have invited Mark to her party? Where was she suddenly finding all this nerve? The spiteful little bitch!

"You and the new boyfriend have other plans, I take it."

"That's right," I agreed, and suddenly found myself adding, "He'll probably want to take me someplace nice for dinner. Maybe even the theater. You know how it is."

"Yeah, too bad there isn't an opera around, with him being so sophisticated," he said sarcastically. "Maybe you'll drive over to Washington and catch the ballet."

"Maybe." I shrugged casually, like there weren't daggers of ice plunging into the region where my heart used to be. "Brad knows a great little French restaurant there."

Mark scowled. "So if you're not planning to be sick with a hangover on Sunday, what are you doing that you need the whole day off for? You can't take off every time the Alfa-Romeo guy crooks his finger at you and says 'jump.' I thought you took this job seriously."

I needed the day off to go with my parents to visit my grandmother for her birthday. But no way was I going to tell him that now. I figured it was time for payback for all those blondes of his and for going to Brenda's party when I couldn't.

"I do take it seriously, you know that," I said. "I wouldn't ask you if it weren't something important." I didn't explain any further. Let him wonder.

"Okay, just this once," he grumbled. "That's our — "

"Yes, I know. Our busiest day."

I had a brief moment of satisfaction when I saw the look on his face. It was obvious he was dying to know what I was doing on Sunday that was so important, but wouldn't let himself ask. Ha! Now he knows what it feels like, I thought.

Of course, that didn't change the fact that I didn't have a fabulous date with a gorgeous guy and his Alfa-Romeo on Sunday. I was going to spend the entire day with my family. And Saturday he'd be at Brenda's party, while I'd be hiding out at my house, watching some old movie on cable and stuffing my face with the kind of food that's murder on your complexion.

Brenda probably had a girl all lined up for him to

meet, a girl she'd met through Peter, like his sister or cousin, or somebody like that. Maybe even somebody really pretty, and older.

I still couldn't believe Brenda could be so mean to me.

I hoped her party was a complete flop. That hardly anybody showed up, and those who did had such a boring time that they left after ten minutes. That they would use her party to measure other boring parties for the next twenty years and say, "Yep! Brenda's party was still the most boring!" *That's* what I hoped.

Saturday night was tough, but Sunday was torture, I swear. Every time I see my grandfather, he always asks me if I have any new boyfriends. Actually, he asks me if I've broken any new hearts. That's exactly the way he puts it, every single time since I was about six years old. Rituals are very important to old people, so usually I just sort of smile and say, "Millions! Simply millions!" He gets a real kick out of it. But this time, when he asked me, I almost started to cry, that's how depressed I was. It really put a damper on things. So I probably ruined my grandmother's birthday, and it was all Brenda's fault. And Mark's, too, of course.

I mean, it's one thing not to have a boyfriend. But not to have a best friend was absolutely the worst. Especially when your best friend has just walked all over you wearing those kinds of spiked heels hookers wear.

Then one evening, later that same week, I was doing my daily routine — shaving my legs. Have you ever noticed how much faster the hair on your legs grows in the summer? Anyway, there was a knock on the bathroom door, and Mom stuck her head in.

"Oh, good, you're not in the shower yet. Mark's here to see you."

"Mark!" I jumped up so fast, I nicked my leg. "Ohmigod!" I dabbed at the blood on my leg and started prancing around. Mark had only been to my house a few times, and then only to drop me off. Of course, he'd met my parents before since his mother and mine are friendly. But to drop by unexpectedly! Boyfriend behavior! Definitely boyfriend behavior!

"Ohmigod!" I said again, running into my room and throwing on my best pair of shorts and a very skimpy top. "Mom, quick, check my back. Do I have any zits?"

"You must be taking lessons from your cousin," my mother said, ignoring my back. "What you're wearing, Norrie! Your father will blow his top!"

"Mom, I haven't got *time* for this now. Do I have any zits or don't I?"

Sighing, she looked over my back. "Not a one. Just some freckles."

I went back to the bathroom and started fiddling with my hair. It was disaster city.

"I'll send him up here, if you want," Mom offered, "as long as you follow the rule about the door staying open."

I thought of my pictures of Mark plastered all over the place, and the calendar where I'd marked every time I'd seen Mark and what I was wearing. My room was out for sure.

"We'll just go out on the patio," I told her, nearly pushing her to get down the stairs. Mom just smiled faintly, looking very motherish as she shook her head.

Mark was downstairs, talking to my father. He actually stood up when I came in. Just like a boyfriend would!

"Look, I'm sorry to drop by unannounced like this — "

"Oh, that's okay — "

"The thing is, I know I should have called first. I thought maybe you'd be going out or something." He looked around, like Brad was suddenly going to materialize. He'd caught me dateless, but I was prepared.

"Well, I have to work early tomorrow, you know."

"Sure." He glanced at my father, who was pretending to read the newspaper. "Look, Norrie," he said quietly, "I need to talk to you — "

"How about something to drink, Mark?" Mom called from the doorway. "Coke? Ginger ale? Iced tea?"

"No, thanks, Mrs. Plimmon" — Mark glanced at me — "Actually I was hoping we could go for a quick ride," he said. "I thought maybe we could go get a soda or something. We wouldn't be home late."

I didn't even bother checking with my parents. "Sure!" I exclaimed, totally forgetting to be cool. Who cared? Things were finally going my way.

We didn't talk much in the car, but I didn't mind. Not talking gave me the chance to memorize every detail of that night, of Mark's car, of what he was wearing and what I was wearing. I wanted to really *savor* the experience, like preserve it forever in the scrapbook of my mind.

We drove out of O.C., inland, away from the water, where there's still a lot of undeveloped land and farms. Of course, even out in the country, they have burger places.

"I'll get it," he told me. "Coke or Sprite? Or do you want something else?"

"No, a Coke is fine," I said, wondering why we just didn't go in. There weren't a lot of people inside, and no one from school, so we'd have privacy. But, then, I thought, it was also pretty private in Mark's car.

I settled back in my seat. I swear, I was purring like a cat. The night was pretty, cooler than usual. I rolled down the windows and enjoyed the breeze.

By the time he came back, I was feeling strangely relaxed. This was kismet, fate. We'd been destined for each other right from the beginning. It was written in the stars, wasn't it? Why be nervous? There was no need to be nervous. I'd finally gotten what I'd set out to get. Now I just had to reel him in.

"It's a beautiful night," I said blissfully. "Don't you wish you had a convertible? Look, it's so clear, you can see the moon and the stars. Usually you can't see both that well at the same time. I guess that's because it's so much darker out here than in town. Of course, it's not as pretty as moonlight on the water, but it comes close, don't you think?"

"Here, take this already," said Mark, and I sighed, accepting the drink. Obviously, moonlight and twinkling stars that had written our destiny didn't hold the same fascination for Mark as it did for me. Still, I could be patient. I *would* be patient. I'd teach Mark to appreciate moonlight and stars and romance. It'd be a piece of cake, considering what I'd just accomplished.

"Listen, I've got something to tell you," announced Mark. He put down his drink and turned to me. "This isn't going to be easy, Norrie. In fact, it's pretty bad. So I want you to prepare yourself, okay?"

My heart started thumping in alarm. "What? What is it?"

"You know that guy — that *man* — you've been seeing?"

"Who? Oh, right. What about him?"

"Norrie, he's *married*."

Nine

Silence. Then, "Did you hear what I said, Norrie?"

I nodded.

"Are you all right?"

I nodded again.

"Well, don't you want to say anything?"

I shrugged helplessly. My brain was working as fast as it could, which wasn't very fast at all.

"I don't know what to say," I stalled.

"It's true, in case you were wondering," he told me earnestly. "I wouldn't tell you unless I were absolutely positive."

"Oh, yes. I believe you."

A look came over Mark's face like something really horrible had just occurred to him. "You didn't already know, by any chance? You wouldn't go out with a married guy on purpose?" He paused. "Would you?"

"No, never!" I exclaimed emphatically. "I'd never, ever — " I took a deep breath. It was too late to go back now. "I'm shocked by the whole thing," I told him. "Really shocked!"

Well, so far I wasn't technically lying. And Mark seemed pleased. "That's what I figured," he said, nodding his head. "You had no idea?"

"No idea."

"Not a clue?"

I shook my head. "None whatsoever."

"The dirty rotten scum!" Mark hit his fist against the dashboard. I bit my lower lip to keep from flinching.

"Uh — how did you find out?"

"I was having dinner with my family over at Fager's Island last night. That creep walks in with this woman on his arm, and she's got a ring on her finger and everything. My sister's friend works there as the hostess, so I asked her about them and she said the reservation was for a Mr. and Mrs."

Thanks, heaps, sister's friend, whoever you are. I hope you work as a hostess at Fager's Island for the *rest of your natural life.* That you'll end your days with varicose veins that look like a road map, that's what I hope.

"Man, I felt like going over and saying something to that SOB!" Mark was saying. "I would have, too, if he'd been alone! But, you know, I didn't see any reason to get the wife involved. After all, she isn't to blame, right?"

If you only knew. Aloud I said, "Well, I'm glad you didn't do anything. That would have been terrible!"

Mark nodded, drumming his fingers against the

steering wheel, following some primitive macho drumbeat in his head, I guess. He looked like he knew in the intelligent, civilized part of him that I was right, but that the other part of him was wishing he'd decked poor, unsuspecting Brad.

"There's a name for sick creeps like that. You know, those perverts who have a thing for young girls. Man, you should have seen the wife! No guy in his right mind would run around on a total babe like that!"

I didn't say anything to this. My brain was taking it all in, but it was way too overstressed to tell me what to do. So I just kept my mouth shut.

"Oh, Christ, I'm sorry," said Mark. "Here I am, rubbing it in, like you aren't hurting enough! Look, if you want to talk about it — "

I shook my head. I definitely did not want to talk about it.

"You don't have to be embarrassed. I know how these things happen. No fooling. My older sister hooked up with this cop her freshman year of college. They went out for *months* before she found out he was married *and* with a kid on the way! She had it pretty bad there for a while."

"Is she okay now?" I asked politely.

"Oh, sure, she got over it. *Everyone* gets over it," he said meaningfully. "So, if you want to talk about it — "

I shook my head again. "No, really, I couldn't. I'm still so shocked. . . ." I bit my lower lip and tried to look like someone who had just received a devastating shock.

"Yeah, I understand," Mark said, very sympathetic.

He even leaned over and patted my hand. "You were pretty heavy with him, huh?"

"Well, no, not really," I replied carefully. "We just went out a couple of times. You know, to the beach, things like that. There were *always* plenty of people around. It was actually kind of *platonic*."

A few days ago I was trying to convince Mark that Brad and I were hot to trot, and now I was telling him we were just friends? His glance was skeptical, to say the least.

"I saw you on the beach with him once. It looked to me like you two were pretty tight."

"Well, it might have *looked* that way."

"Yeah, and I also heard you and Mr. Adonis were playing tennis together almost every day. I wonder how he got away from his wife?"

"Let's not talk about it," I said quickly, and Mark looked instantly contrite.

"Oh, yeah, sorry. Here I am rambling on like an insensitive jerk — you'd probably like to be alone, right? I'll take you home."

That was probably a good idea, but now that I was finally out with Mark, I couldn't let him go. Besides, my brain was starting to work again, telling my mouth what to say.

"Well, no, actually I'd kind of like some company. That is, unless you're busy — "

"No, I'm easy."

"See, I'm still kind of in shock," I said, and he put his hand over mine again.

"Norrie, it's *okay*," he said softly. "You don't have to explain it to me. My sister, remember?"

I smiled gratefully.

So this is how I got my first date — we went out for ice cream — with Mark. I know it was tricky and sneaky. I know I should have braced myself and told him the truth. I know this because inside, I'm basically a good person, really I am.

But I also know, without a shadow of a doubt, that if I'd told him the truth, he'd have never spoken to me again. I'd have been left at the McDonald's on Route 50, and my mother would have had to come pick me up. And I would have been crying and then I'd have had to explain why I was crying, and I'd have been so humiliated, on top of having just lost Mark for good. So I didn't tell him the truth. I was sneaky and tricky instead.

As it was, I had to call my mom to tell her I'd be a little late. I also tried to call Steff, but, as luck would have it, she wasn't home. I was going to have to wing it alone.

"You did exactly the right thing," said Steff when I told her the next day. "I'm really proud of you, cuz. I don't think I could have handled it better myself."

"I don't know," I said doubtfully. "We spent the entire evening talking or not talking about this supposed relationship I had with a married man. Steff, I think he thinks I had an affair with Brad! No kidding! I'm telling you, he must be fixated on what happened to his sister. He told me the whole story about her, you know, and now he thinks I'm just like her. I told him and told him it wasn't anything that serious, but he wouldn't believe me." I sighed. "It's like I'm this month's charity case for him."

"Stop complaining. At least it's a start."

"Yeah? And what if he finds out the truth?"

"How's he going to do that? Brad's left already."

"*You're* still here, and you're not exactly the forgettable type, you know. Anyway, Brad'll be back."

Steffie just shrugged, turning over in the sand. We were on the beach by her mother's house again; Steffie aiming for the perfect tan, me sitting up, sifting sand through my fingers, thinking about the night before. My first date with Mark, and we'd spent all of it talking about another man!

A shadow fell upon my face, and I looked up to see a well-built guy about twenty-five grinning at Steff. "Would you girls like a beer?" he asked. "My friend and I got plenty to spare."

"No, we would not," I told him firmly.

"Just as well, I don't want to be arrested for contributing to the delinquency of a minor," he said, giving me a jeering glance before getting back to Steff. "But why don't you let your sister speak for herself?"

"She's my cousin and she's — "

" — not really into beer," Steffie finished for me. I stared at her, openmouthed. She had to have known I was about to tell the guy that she was married!

"What kind of things are you into?" he asked, reminding me of that other jerk, Rick. They both had the same *insinuating* style, like what they're saying isn't necessarily what they're meaning.

If I'd been Steff, with a terrific husband, I would have told this jerk that it was none of his damned business what kind of things I was into, but Steff didn't say anything at all. She just shrugged and looked mysterious. The guy grinned.

A few feet away, a couple of other guys were waving in our direction. "Your buddies want you," I told him. He looked over at them briefly and then back to Steff in all her glory.

"Gotta go. Maybe we'll see you around later?"

"Maybe," she agreed, smiling. I just glared at him.

"Steff, what is the matter with you?" I demanded as he trotted back to his beer-guzzling buddies. "Why didn't you tell that creep you were married?"

"It's really not that big a deal, Norrie."

"But he thought you were available!" I protested.

"Who cares what he thought? Chill out, will you? I only said three words — "

"Five words."

"Okay, five words to the guy. That isn't a crime, you know."

"But if Brad knew — "

"Brad isn't here," she snapped, turning away from me. "He's miles away, and I'm bored, bored, *bored*. This summer isn't turning out at all like I thought it would."

I stared at her, confused. Bored? How could Steffie possibly be bored? Between working in Aunt Caroline's shop, seeing all her old friends, not to mention me, when I could manage it — well, Steffie just didn't have *time* to be bored, that's all there was to it.

When I got home there was a message on our machine from Mark. He sounded so serious that I called him back right away, not even changing out of my bathing suit first.

"Are you okay?" he asked, first thing.

"I'm fine," I said.

He didn't believe me. "No, seriously, how're you doing?"

"Seriously, I'm doing fine."

"Well . . . if you need to talk — "

"Thanks, Mark." I sighed. "You're really sweet."

"What are friends for? Think of it as an employee benefit. One strong shoulder, dry shirt, ready to cry on any time you want."

But I don't want to *cry* on your shoulder, I thought. Snuggle, lay my head on it, yes, yes, yes! But no crying!

"You shouldn't stay at home moping all the time," he said, forgetting that I hadn't been home when he'd called earlier. "You should try to get out more."

"I'm not moping," I protested. "I've just come back from the beach, as a matter of fact."

"Who'd you go with?"

"My cousin." Did he think I'd been with Brad?

"Good, good," he said heartily. "It's good to get out, you know, to get your mind off things." There was a pause. "Are you going out tonight?"

My heart started thumping. Oh, please, let this be what I think it is. "Well, I haven't made any plans. Why?"

"Nothing. Well, I was wondering if maybe you'd like to see a movie. That always works for me when I feel down, you know? There's that Tom Cruise movie at the mall. Want to see it?"

Was the Pope Catholic? Did a bear — ?

"Arrghuhuoundsgud," I replied. Thankfully, he took it for an affirmative.

"All right, then. I'll pick you up around seven."

Watching a Tom Cruise movie with O.C.'s very own Tom Cruise look-alike. A dream come true. Yeah, this was it, I thought, with deep satisfaction. Who cared if I'd already seen it? A dark theater, a romantic movie with plenty of love scenes. Bingo!

I didn't pay much attention to the movie. I didn't need to since I'd already seen it, right? So I concentrated on Mark. Every time there was a romantic moment on screen, I would hold my breath, waiting for him to kiss me, put his arm around my shoulders, *anything*. It was time to share some tender moments of our own. But the only thing we shared was a bucket of popcorn.

"Great movie," said Mark as they rolled the credits. "You like it?"

"Oh, yes, loved it." I blinked my eyes as the lights suddenly came back on. Not for the first time I thought that theaters are way too quick to put the lights back on. They ought to give you more of a chance to get used to the change from dark to bright. They ought to try to lead you more gently back from the magical world of the movie to the reality of the smelly theater with very sticky floors.

"People probably have told you this before," I said shyly. "But you sort of look like Tom Cruise."

"Get real."

"No, really, you could be his younger brother."

"That's rich!" He laughed. "No, no one's ever told me that before. But I tell you, I wish — "

" — you had his money, right?"

"That, too," he agreed. "But I was going to say I wish I had his opportunities with girls."

Privately, I thought Mark did well enough on his own with girls; he didn't need Tom Cruise's, too. Besides, there was this perfectly nice girl right next to him, just ripe for the picking, so to speak.

We ran into Brenda and Peter outside the theater. Brenda looked at me and Mark. *Surprise, surprise!* I looked at her. *So there!* Then we exchanged stiff, phony smiles. You know the kind I mean.

Peter, meanwhile, was greeting us like we were all long-lost siblings or something. I mean, I hardly know the guy.

"Hey, I thought that was you, Bishop!" he exclaimed. "You two want to go get a slice with Brenda and me?"

It was hard to say who looked more horrified — Brenda or me.

"Oh, Peter — " she began.

"Well — " I started.

"Thanks, anyway," Mark's voice overrode us all. "We have something else planned."

I breathed with relief. Peter, of course, couldn't let it go. "Sorry we missed you at the party last week, Norrie," he told me. "Brenda said you had something else to do. Maybe next time you can bring him along."

"Maybe." I looked at Brenda. So she told him *everything,* did she? Ha!

Peter kept blabbing for a few more minutes before Brenda finally dragged him away. Then Mark and I started walking back to his car.

"Peter's a nice guy, but he sure does talk a lot," I said. "You wouldn't believe how much shyer he was when we first met him."

"Hmmm."

"You never did tell me, did you have a good time at Brenda's party?"

105

He shrugged. "It was okay."

Ha! So Brenda's party hadn't been a complete success! That was good to know, even though it didn't give me as much pleasure as I would have thought. The truth was, I really missed Brenda.

"I hope you didn't mind me answering for you back there," Mark said. "I could tell that you didn't really feel comfortable with them."

"Oh." Mark must have sensed that Brenda and I were fighting. Good thing he didn't know what we'd been fighting about. "Well, it's nothing major," I said airily and as soon as I'd said it, I realized it was true. Brenda and I would be making up soon.

"Come on, Norrie, it was obvious you didn't want to be with them. I guess the jealousy thing is hard to handle, huh?"

"Say what?"

"You know, with her being your best friend, and the two of them so cutesy together. Makes it kind of tough for you, being around a happy couple so soon after — " he gestured the rest.

I sighed. Here we go again! "Mark, it's okay. Really it is. I can take it."

"You don't have to put up a front with me, Norrie. Even though I admire you for trying, believe me, it's not good to keep it all in."

I gave up. This was too bizarre for words. Mark had turned from a nice, normal American boy who loved taking pictures into Dr. Freud. Life was throwing me another curveball.

"Listen, are you in a hurry to get home?" I asked. "You've been so nice to me, and so understanding — I'd like to take *you* out."

"Aw, you don't have to do that, Norrie."

"No, really, I want to. Maybe some ice cream? On me?"

So we drove down to the boardwalk and walked up to where the action is, where the music blares and the smell of Dolly's Caramel Corn is everywhere. By then we were hungry for some real food. I bought a burger for each of us and a large order of fries for Mark.

Then we walked into the video arcade. I don't normally like video games, but all guys, no matter what their age, really get off on the things. That's a fact. So I bought us three dollars' worth of quarters. They didn't last very long, because we were playing the expensive games. But at least Mark wasn't talking about Brad anymore. He seemed more relaxed, and our date began to feel more like a *date* and not like a session at the shrink's office.

After the video arcade, we drifted into the amusement park area. My favorite ride, the one I was really hoping he'd want to go on, is the kiddie Ferris wheel. There's a very good reason why I was so partial to that Ferris wheel, and why I much preferred it to the bigger, scarier one. See, I'd once watched this movie where a girl and guy take the Ferris wheel and kiss just as they get to the top. It is super-romantic up there because it's quiet, and the view is pretty, and the mechanic operating the Ferris wheel usually gives everyone a few minutes at the top.

The small Ferris wheel is also my favorite because it doesn't tip you upside down or go around too fast. Once, when I was a little girl, I'd thrown up on the Himalaya. Since then I've avoided those kinds of rides but good. Even if Mark had suggested we go on the Himalaya, I would have had to say no. Especially since we'd just had greasy boardwalk hamburgers. Sure, I wanted to please the guy, but I'd already thrown up on him once. No need to repeat the experience.

Luckily, there were long lines outside all of those rides, so we ended up with bumper cars instead. That was fun, even though I was nervous. I've never been very good at bumper cars, which kind of makes me wonder how I'll do at driving next March when I turn sixteen.

"Crazy women drivers!" Mark shouted when I'd backed my car into a corner and couldn't get out. He had to come help me, but he didn't seem mad. He was grinning and he even patted me on the shoulder, which got me so flustered I nearly ran him over before he could get back into his car.

"Hey, when you get your license, tell me, okay?" he yelled. "I want to make sure I move out of the state!"

But he was still grinning when he said that, so I guess it was okay.

We never got to the Ferris wheel. We did walk out on the pier, though, which would have been romantic if there hadn't been so many people around. As usual, the boardwalk around First Street was a mob scene. And why did they need so many electric lights? Didn't the city know that was a needless waste of money?

The pier runs through this humongous water slide. I mean, the most excellent water slide you've ever seen. Mark bought us two ice-cream cones, and we walked out underneath it, and toward the water. Fantastic.

We talked, really talked. I mean, we were finally having one of those meaningful conversations I'd dreamed about so often. We talked about school, about photography, about music we liked, even about *books* we liked, if you can believe that.

And even if he didn't hold my hand or kiss me or anything, I was supremely happy. The kissing would come in time, I was sure. For now, I was near him and that was enough.

We had to kind of hurry it on home, because I was in danger of not making curfew. He got to my door with just three minutes to spare.

"Thanks," I said, glancing at him in the darkness. God, what a profile!

"Thank *you*," he said, and we sort of laughed. You know, those half-laughs when something isn't that funny, but you feel like you have to do *something*.

"I had a really great time," I told him shyly.

"Me, too." He sounded surprised when he said that, but there was a lilt in his voice that let me know it had been a *pleasant* surprise.

Briefly I considered leaning over and kissing him on the cheek, since he obviously wasn't going to make the first move. Did I have the guts?

"You'd better get going if you're going to make curfew," he reminded me.

"Uh — right." I didn't have the guts. "Well, thanks. See you."

"See you," he returned, and then I got out of the car. He didn't pull out of the driveway until I'd opened the door to our house and was almost inside.

I waved at him before I went inside, but it was too dark to see if he waved back. But I think he did.

I floated upstairs to my room. I kissed each photo of Mark before going to bed. I always kissed them before going to bed, but this time I kissed them *with feeling.*

Ten

Tuesday morning, the crack of dawn; I was anxiously peering through the living room blinds, waiting for Mark. I ran out of the house even before his car pulled into the driveway. I didn't want to wake my parents.

"Hi," he greeted me. His face had a soft and fuzzy morning look. I could see signs of where he'd recently cut himself shaving. Mark *shaved!* "You got everything?" he asked.

"Yes." We were going over to Assateague Island to take some photos. Assateague is basically a pile of sand with a herd of wild ponies running around. But there are lots of photo opportunities, and it's quiet. Almost nobody goes there.

"Bathing suit? Extra film?"

"Plus food," I said. "Everything we need."

There was a flash of white teeth. "I don't function

as well as you this early in the morning. I forgot my 200 millimeter lens. We'll have to swing by my house to pick it up, okay?"

"Sure." I smiled back at him. "No problem."

"It's going to be a great day," he said, backing up the car.

"Totally great," I agreed. Outside, the dawn was slowly breaking its way through the darkness; it looked like God was painting the sky with tiny strokes of pinkish-gray. Beautiful. I glanced over at Mark's profile. Also beautiful, in a strong kind of way. I sighed. A whole, complete day together. Starting now. Very, very beautiful.

It was a short distance to Mark's house. We let ourselves in very quietly. He didn't want to wake up his parents, either. Mark's room was on the ground floor.

"It's a mess, but come on in," he said, switching on the light. He made a dive toward the bedclothes, straightening them, I guess. I appreciated him making the effort, not that I was really noticing the bed. My eyes were fixed on the walls. They were covered with photographs from top to bottom. Every spare inch. Most of them looked too old to be his.

"Unbelievable!" I exclaimed wonderingly. "And I thought *I* had a collection."

"I've been at it a lot longer than you," he reminded me. "Like them?"

"I love them. Totally unbelievable."

Mark went into the bathroom, or what I thought was a bathroom. He'd made it into a darkroom. Talk about dedication to your art! Imagine having your own

112

private bathroom and giving it up just to have a dark-room!

"It'll only take me a minute," he called.

"Take your time," I answered.

Just then my eyes focused on a female nude. Okay, the picture was artsy, in black and white, of course, and it was shot through sheer fabric. But it was still a naked woman, and those were her *breasts*. I turned away from that one quickly, just as he came back into the room.

What would his parents think if they came in here and saw me standing in their son's bedroom, looking at photos of nude women? I had a good idea what *my* parents would think. I felt myself start to blush.

It's a funny thing about blushing: The more you tell yourself not to, the more you do it. I was sure Mark was going to notice and think I was really childish. I mean, why be embarrassed, right? This woman might be proportioned a little differently from me, but, basically, she didn't have anything I didn't have.

Thinking that, I felt kind of exposed, and that's when I started to seriously turn red. I bent down and pretended to study another black-and-white photo. This one was of a sad-looking woman with two dirty children.

"Dorothea Lange," Mark said, coming up beside me. "She worked for the government during the Depression, taking photos of the poor and homeless. There were a whole bunch of them doing that, but she was the best by far. Excellent, huh?"

"No, it's sad," I told him. "They look so hungry."

"They were."

I glanced around the room. "You seem to like depressing subjects."

"That's what photojournalism is all about. Realism. Making people feel something. Making them see how things really are."

"I don't think I want to know how things really are. Like that one — " I pointed to a black-and-white older photo of a lone soldier on a battlefield. His arms were flung out, and his head was back, like he'd just been hit with a bullet. "I think maybe that's too realistic."

"Are you serious?" he demanded. "That's probably the most famous war photograph of all time. It was taken during the Spanish Civil War. The photographer had to get into one of the dugouts so he could get the shot at the exact instant the soldier was killed."

"You mean, he took it on purpose? He set it up deliberately?"

"Well, he didn't shoot the guy himself, you know. But he put himself where he knew there'd be plenty of action, sure."

"That's pretty sick, Mark."

"War is sick — that's what he wanted to show. Robert Capa was the greatest war photographer *ever*. He took risks like you wouldn't believe. He covered practically every war of this century. He finally got killed in Vietnam. Stepped on a land mine."

I took a closer look. The soldier was young, maybe not so much older than Mark. And now he was dead. He'd been dead a long time, but once he'd been our age. I felt this sort of shudder go through me. Mark must have noticed.

"That's just the reaction Capa was aiming for," he

said approvingly. "First you're shocked. Then you feel. And then — hopefully — you think."

"Don't you have any happy pictures?" I asked. I thought about my collection of children, animals, rock musicians, and movie stars. "You know, like celebrities, stuff like that?"

He laughed, but it wasn't a sneering kind of laugh. "I leave that to you paparazzi people," he said. "Come on, you can look at these another time. We gotta get out of here if we're going to catch the light."

Another time? That was a very positive sign. I felt my heart do a little dance as I followed him out the door.

I could smell fresh coffee brewing. Even though I don't like to drink it much, I usually love the smell of coffee. Not today, though, because I knew it must mean that Mark's parents were up.

We walked right into the kitchen. Just as I'd feared, Mr. and Mrs. Bishop were there, fixing breakfast. They were still in their robes, even. They didn't act too surprised to see a girl coming out of their son's bedroom at the crack of dawn.

"Hey, son, I thought you were going to get an early start," said Mr. Bishop, pouring orange juice. He smiled at me, his eyes crinkling at the corners just like Mark's do. I smiled back, feeling kind of embarrassed. Mr. Bishop's robe was open at the front, and he had a *lot* of chest hair. Was Mark going to have hair like that one day? Maybe even on his back? God, I hoped not.

"We had to come back for something," said Mark. "You guys know Norrie, don't you?"

"Of course. Good morning, Norrie," said Mrs. Bishop. "How's your mother?"

Why was she asking about my mother? What did she *really* want to know?

"She's fine, thanks," I said.

"Would you like some juice or something to eat?" she asked.

What does she think I've been doing that I need to eat again? "No, thanks. I just had breakfast a few minutes ago." I accentuated the *few minutes* part, just in case she was getting any ideas. "I'm full, couldn't eat another bite," I added.

"And we're outta here," Mark said, taking my hand. "Say good-bye, Norrie."

"Good-bye," I parroted. "Nice seeing you!"

"Have a good day," Mrs. Bishop called.

"Watch out for sharks," Mr. Bishop added. Don't ask me what he meant by that, because I have no idea. It's taken me years just to figure out my own parents, you know?

Mark held onto my hand until we got to the door. I estimated that was about thirty seconds of hand-holding. Maybe even more. Who cared about his parents? My day with Mark had just begun, and already he'd held my hand for more than half a minute!

As soon as we got to Assateague, we started walking away from the public areas and toward the north end of the island. Mark wanted to take some pictures of the inlet between Assateague and Ocean City. Once, a long time ago, the two had been just one island. Then a really ferocious hurricane had separated them forever. The inlet was at least five miles away, so I didn't see how we were going to make it there and back in one day. Walking long distances in sand is really tough, even when you're used to it like we are.

We walked and walked, constantly on the lookout for some of these supposed wild ponies. I'd seen them before, so I knew for a fact that they existed. The ones in the parking lot mooching around for handouts didn't count, of course.

Meanwhile, Mark was taking pictures of everything that moved. I swear, the guy must have been Japanese in another life. There's no other explanation. He took pictures of sand patterns, of birds, he even took pictures of this shark's head that had washed up on the beach. It was totally repulsive, and I couldn't understand why anyone would want a photo of *that*.

"It's repulsive, but interesting," Mark insisted. "Some fisherman must have thrown it overboard."

I was about to ask him why anyone would do such a disgustingly gross thing, when a herd of ponies started galloping toward us. It was like they'd come out of nowhere. Sand was flying, I was struggling with my camera, and meanwhile, Mark was click, click, clicking away like a maniac. They had passed us in a matter of minutes, their hooves thundering across the sand.

"Excellent!" Mark shouted, grinning at me. "Did you get any decent shots?"

"Maybe two at the most. You wouldn't think they could move so fast, would you?"

"Yeah," he agreed, but I could tell his mind was already on the great photos he'd be developing later. Sighing, my eyes followed the ponies, who were slowing down about half a mile away. Even from this distance, their bodies looked shorter and sturdier than normal horses', and their hair was coarse and matted from living on an island that's bitterly cold and windy in the winter and hot and mosquito-ridden in the summer. Not exactly paradise, but the ponies had done all right for themselves.

They started playing around — horsing around? — with each other, or at least that's what I thought it was at first. Then the bully of the group started biting at this golden-colored one. After a few nips, the golden one decided he wasn't going to take it anymore and started kicking his hind legs.

"Are they going to fight?" I asked. Mark was still shooting, using his longest telephoto lens.

He grinned. "No, I think that's just the stallion keeping his harem in line."

"You mean the bully is the male?"

"He's not a bully — he just has to get tough once in a while. How else is he supposed to manage six mares all on his own?"

"Someone ought to tell them about women's liberation," I muttered, pushing my fingers through my hair to get it off my neck. God, it was *hot*. We'd been walking for at least two hours. I could feel the sweat starting to trickle down my spine. Under my too-tight shorts, the bottom of my suit was sliding up the crack of my rear, and that's not the kind of thing you can adjust without anybody noticing.

"Can we stop yet?" I asked and, to my total surprise, Mark agreed.

"But, first, do that thing with your hair again," he said. "It was great. The sun really picks up the highlights when you do that."

Smiling at him, I did as he asked. He shook his

head. "No, Norrie, not like that. Look natural. Like I'm not even here."

Considering he was less than a foot away from me, I thought this was a totally unreasonable request. But I tried anyway.

"That's better," he said, clicking away. "You know, you could be a model."

I tried not to look too pleased. "Really?"

"Sure. You take direction easily. Very important."

I noticed he didn't say anything about my looks. I decided he was going to pay for that.

We set our stuff down and started to strip down to our suits. The moment of truth had arrived.

I'd gotten myself a new two-piece just for the occasion. It was green and pink, with a strapless top and a very high-cut bottom. After all the walking I'd done, my legs were looking good, even if my butt was a little on the large side. The style of the bottom camouflaged it pretty well and, besides, there were a lot of butts bigger than mine. Overall, I was pleased with the way I looked in it. But the real question was how Mark would react.

I turned. He looked at me. I looked at him. Usually Mark wore Jams. That day he was wearing what Brenda and I call "ball-slingers," for very obvious reasons. You know, those little European jobs that don't leave a whole lot to the imagination. So immediately I noticed that Mark has got this little trail of dark hair starting at his belly-button and going all the way down to where his itsy-bitsy suit started. It probably goes all the way down to his you-know-what. God, I could feel myself start to turn red again, and I swear, it had nothing to do with the sun.

"Last one in is a rotten egg!" I called and started to run, totally forgetting my resolution to never give Mark a view of the butt. Oh, well, maybe he wouldn't get past the legs.

We splashed around in the water and then we started to bodysurf. Only I don't do it right, so you can't call it bodysurfing. I just let the wave carry me any which way and hope I don't drown.

Mark took hold of my hand a few times, and once when we were under the waves, I felt something brush past my breast. I think it must have been Mark. I wondered if he did it on purpose. I wondered why he just didn't kiss me and get it over with. The suspense was killing me.

He got out of the water before I did. I could see him reaching for his camera and his zoom lens. I knew he was taking pictures of me again, so I tried to act as natural as possible. But it's hard, let me tell you. I kept pulling up my top and hoping my hair didn't look too awful.

He was still shooting as I came toward the towel. I made a face at him.

"Okay, okay, I get the message," he said, putting his camera down. "Are you hungry?"

"Starving. I thought you'd never ask."

We put all our food out, most of which was pretty heavy in the sugar department — for quick energy, of course. We devoured it all. Considering the amount of exercise we'd done, I figured it was okay if we ate like pigs.

When our stomachs were full, we started to feel kind of sleepy. The sun can do that to you, you know. So we leaned back and soaked up the rays.

"Yeah, this is what it's all about," said Mark, shutting his eyes. "The sun, the beach, the waves — "

" — the pony manure."

"Nice, Norrie, really nice." He opened his eyes and looked over at me. "You know what I think?"

"What?"

"I think we ought to do this more often."

I think you ought to kiss me.

"Do what more often?" I asked.

"You know, get out, enjoy ourselves more. It's too much work, work, work, all the time. Smelling the roses and all that stuff — it's what being young is all about, right? Sometimes you just gotta relax a little."

"Relax? You call what we've been doing today relaxing? Running around in ninety-degree weather, swatting mosquitoes, photographing everything in sight — this is the first time you've relaxed all day!"

He propped himself up on one elbow and looked directly at me. I swear, my heart stopped beating for about thirty seconds. I was definitely not relaxed.

"You telling me it hasn't been fun?"

"No, it's been fun," I agreed huskily. "Real fun."

"Yeah." He sighed, turning his face to the sun. "We'll do it again, okay?"

"Okay." I smiled. He smiled. Okay, we're both smiling. Now all we have to do is lean over just a little bit and . . .

Mark looked down and starting poking at the sand with his fingers. "Listen, Norrie, there's something I've been meaning to ask you. You know, about this married guy you were seeing."

I could have screamed. Absolutely screamed. "Do we have to talk about him again?"

"Well, not if it makes you uncomfortable."

"It doesn't make me uncomfortable, it just makes me bored. I mean, it's not like it was any big thing, you know. I've practically forgotten him." *Forgive me, Brad.*

"I guess you haven't had any really big things."

"What do you mean?"

"You know, a serious boyfriend. Long-term. At least, I never noticed you dating anybody at school seriously."

"You, neither," I said defensively. Of course I hadn't dated anyone seriously. I'm in love with you, you idiot!

"I don't like to get too serious," Mark said.

"Me, neither," I lied.

"Best to keep it light," he shrugged. "You know."

"Definitely. I couldn't agree more." I couldn't be lying more, but what else could I do? If I told the truth, Mark would be running for the parking lot, screaming for his life.

"So, anyway — " he began and frowned. A shadow had crossed his face. It was from a cloud, blocking out the sun.

"So, anyway," I prompted, but Mark wasn't paying attention. My eyes followed his up to the sky, which was fast turning from blue to gray.

Startled, I looked down to the other end of the island, where the sky was nearly black with dark, angry clouds. And they were coming this way, racing across the sky just like a herd of wild ponies.

"Mark — " I began uneasily, and then we saw the flash of lightning.

Eleven

Mark was already getting our stuff together. "Come on, let's get out of here," he said, pulling on his shorts. "There was a house a couple of miles back."

"Can we make it?" I asked. There was another flash of lightning. It seemed closer this time.

"We're going to try," he said, throwing my stuff at me. "Come on, Norrie, we have to get going *now*."

I hurriedly got my clothes on. I knew why Mark was sounding so worried. There are no trees on Assateague. We were the tallest things on the beach, the most likely target for the lightning that seemed to be getting closer every second. I was plenty worried, too.

The sky opened up, and suddenly it was pouring. Mark grabbed my hand, and we made for the dunes. Over to our right I saw a group of ponies galloping toward the bushes. The sight of them almost stopped me, but Mark just kept pushing me on.

Inside my head I could hear my feet pounding over the soft, sinking sand, but outside all I heard was the rain and the thunder. Within minutes we were soaking wet, and my sides ached from the effort of running.

"Come on, Norrie, hurry!" Mark shouted, pulling my arm. I tried to keep up with him, but my legs were already buckling underneath me.

Ca-rack! I jumped as a jagged bolt lit across the sky. The noise was deafening. It practically shook the island.

"It's getting closer, Mark!"

"Don't stop!" he ordered, dragging me behind him. "Run, Norrie, run!"

"I can't — run — any — faster," I panted, holding my sides. *Ca-rack!* Another lightning bolt hit the island. "Mark!" I shrieked. "It's right on top of us. We're going to get hit!"

"No, we're not! Now come on!" he said furiously. "What the hell are you doing?"

I ignored him. I was busy counting the seconds between the flash and the sound. I knew five seconds equaled a mile. "One, two, three — "

"*Come on,* Norrie!"

"four, five, si — "

Ca-rack!

"It's only a mile away!" I shouted at him through the rain. "We're not going to make it in time!"

Ca-rack!

I screamed, covering my ears with my hands as I fell to the ground. I didn't mean to, but it was so *loud.* We had to do something fast, or else I knew we were going to fry. But what? We couldn't make it to the house, and there was absolutely no other place to hide.

"I'm scared, Mark! What are we going to do?"

Mark looked at me, then around the beach, like he expected another house to suddenly materialize. Then he started pulling me between two sand dunes.

"Lie down, Norrie!" he ordered. "Lie down, now!"

Ca-rack! I screamed again. Mark pushed me down, and my body hit the sand with a thud. I felt the sand in my mouth, mingling with the rain. My hair was all wet and tangled in my face, and I tried to get it out of my eyes so that I could see.

"We're going to die, Mark!"

"We're not going to die," he shouted, pushing my head down so hard, he could have broken my neck. "So shut up and *keep your head down!*"

I felt his arm around me and realized he was trying to cover my body with his. His leg was on top of me, and he was patting my shoulder. But I could tell by his voice that he was scared, too.

Ca-rack! Mark gripped me tighter, so tight I couldn't breath for a few seconds. We were both shaking, and I think his teeth were chattering even more than mine. There were flashing lights all around us, and the noise made my eardrums hurt. It was like we were suddenly caught in the middle of a war, Beirut or someplace like that, with guns and bombs going off in every direction. It seemed to go on for hours. It seemed like the end of the world had come.

"Don't worry, we're going to get through this," Mark shouted in my ear. I tried to open my eyes. His face was right on top of mine, but all I could see were his lips. They were moving. At first I thought he was trying to say something to me, and then I realized that he was praying.

I should pray, too, I thought, and tried to remember some of the prayers I'd learned back in Sunday school. If only I'd gone to church more often! I'd learned plenty of prayers, but the only one I could remember was the one that went, "If I should die before I wake, I pray the Lord my soul to take." It went around and around in my head, even though I was trying like hell to think of something that didn't mention dying. Finally I gave up trying to remember prayers. God wouldn't hold a bad memory against me at a time like this, would he?

"I don't want to die, God, please don't let me die," I mumbled. "Please, God, please, don't let us die."

Somehow I found Mark's hand and I held on to it, gripping it like a lifeline through all that terrifying racket. Maybe the force of our combined prayers would help. God wouldn't let the both of us die, not yet, not yet, please, God, not yet. Please let me live a little while longer first. I'm still a virgin! Please, God, don't let us die, *please!*

There was another *ca-rack!* and I felt Mark's fingers move in mine. All around us was this strange *bzzz-zip, bzzz-zip* noise. It was like that noise you get when you try to brush your hair and there's too much static electricity, only much, much louder. It was followed by a blinding white flash and the biggest, loudest, most violent *ca-rack!* ever.

Suddenly I wasn't thinking anymore, or praying. I just stopped. Everything just stopped. The end had come; the world went dark and quiet.

• • •

I woke up about a minute later — or at least I *think* it was about a minute later. I nudged Mark next to me. He didn't move. I turned his face toward me, my heart pounding away in sick fear. Mark's eyes were closed, and his lips weren't moving anymore.

"Mark! Wake up, Mark!" I shouted, shaking him. "Wake up, wake up!" I shook him again — hard — and harder still. But his eyes wouldn't open. I tried to see if he was still breathing. I put my head down on his chest to hear his heartbeat, but I couldn't hear anything through all the rain and the *bzzz-zip, bzzz-zip* noise.

"Oh, God, please don't be dead," I cried weakly. What was I supposed to do now? Mouth to mouth? Would it do any good? I didn't even know how you were supposed to do it! Why hadn't I taken CPR along with Brenda when the school offered it last fall?

"Goddammit, Mark, wake up!" I screamed, shaking him hard. I even slapped him on the face. But he just lay there, looking and feeling dead. The water fell cold and hard on my face as I howled with frustration at my own helplessness. I didn't know what else to do.

I would never forgive myself, never, ever, *ever*. This was all my fault to begin with. If I'd run faster, if I hadn't let him try to protect me. That's why he was dead, and he didn't even know how much I loved him.

I started sobbing over him, telling him how much I loved him, praying and pleading with him to live, when suddenly, just like a miracle, his eyes fluttered open and he stared at me.

"Didn't I tell you to keep your head down?" he

demanded in this perfectly normal voice. That's when I really lost it. Mark blinked. Poor guy — to wake up from the dead to find this hysterical girl slobbering all over him.

"Shh, it's okay, Norrie, it's okay, now," he said, patting my shoulder awkwardly. "Jesus! That last bolt was too close for comfort, huh? It must have knocked us out — how long do you think? Maybe a couple of minutes?" He cocked his head to get a look at the sky. "The rain is slowing down."

I looked up, too. He was right. It wasn't raining so hard anymore. The thunder was moving away, too.

"Hey, what are you crying about?" he asked. "You're not hurt, are you?"

Wordlessly I shook my head.

"It's all over, and we made it. I told you we would, didn't I?"

I had to hit him. I swear, he deserved it. He deserved a few very bad curse words, too. "I thought you were *dead*!" I told him furiously.

"Hey, I'm sorry to disappoint you, but I'm alive."

"It's not funny! Don't you dare laugh at me!" I saw that grin creep across his face and I punched him in the arm. "You scared me out of my mind! I woke up, you were dead, and I knew it was *all my fault*!"

"It wouldn't have been your fault. But, Norrie, I'm not dead. See?" He thumped himself on the chest. "I'm here, in the flesh, so you have nothing to worry about."

I wiped my hand across my face and glared at him. "I've never been so scared in my life!"

"Yeah, I know. Me, too," he admitted. "But it's over, Norrie, so you can stop crying now, okay?"

So of course I started to cry harder, and then my head was on his shoulder, and he was holding me like a child. I didn't mind. It felt good. Really good. I pounded my fist against his shoulder one more time for good measure, but only half-heartedly. I was too happy he was alive to be mad at him.

"Shhh, sweetheart, it's okay," he muttered, holding my fist. "It's okay, now, Norrie. Please don't cry, sweetheart. Come on, enough already, okay? Or else you're gonna make me cry, too."

"Maybe we are dead." My voice was muffled against his chest, but he heard me. I could tell by the way he stopped moving that he'd heard me. "Maybe we're dead and we just don't know it," I said, pulling away.

He shook his head, but he looked uneasy. That got me scared all over again. I hadn't really meant it, but now that I thought about it, maybe it was true. "How do you know we're not dead?" I persisted. "We don't know what being dead is like!"

And suddenly his arms were around me, and he was kissing me. It came out of nowhere, like in a movie, or in a dream. He was kissing me and he felt so sure, so strong, that I felt sure and strong, too. I couldn't be dead. Dead people didn't feel, they didn't taste. Mark tasted salty, like the sea and my tears mixed together. He smelled like cold rain and sweat. His lips weren't cold, though; they were warm and slightly rough from the sand that still clung to them.

Both of us were kind of wobbly by the time we pulled apart, but it was a good kind of wobbly. "I thought we were going to die," I whispered against his neck. "I thought we were going to die without me having the chance to tell you how I really feel."

"I know, Norrie," he said, hugging me. "Me, too."
I felt his body shiver, and knew that this was real.
This was really happening. He kissed me again, and
it seemed to go on and on forever. On the other hand,
it seemed to end much too soon. But Mark's arms were
still around me, and that felt good.

"The rain's stopped," I said.

"Hmmm, about time," he muttered, rubbing his
hands over my arms. "Are you okay now? Still cold?"

I shook my head. "Not as much as before."

He brushed the hair out of my face. "Did you know
that you have one green eye? I never noticed that
before."

"Do you mind?"

"No, I like it." He kissed the corner of my eye
lightly, the way a butterfly would kiss. "It's kind of
sexy."

I smiled. "Did you know that you have freckles
across your nose? Not many, just a few."

"Mind?"

"No. They're kind of sexy, too." Mark could even
make freckles look sexy. It figured.

He grinned, flashing those dimples that, just minutes ago, I thought I'd never see again. It's funny how
things work out, you know? Funny and wonderful.

Thank you, God.

"Come on." Mark took my hand. "Let's get the hell
out of here."

I stumbled as he was helping me up, and he winced
with pain. "What's the matter?" I asked. "Are you
hurt?"

"My neck and back are pretty sore. Also, my head
is pounding. What about you?"

"My foot, I guess." I was looking at it in surprise, because it was the first time I'd noticed that it was throbbing. "It feels like I twisted it or something."

"That must have been the part of you that was exposed," he said, rubbing his head.

"Are you sure you're okay?" I asked. "You were the one who really got it the worst."

He smiled, but it was a pretty grim smile. "I don't mind. Now I know for sure we're not dead. You don't have pain in heaven, right?"

I smiled back. "Maybe we didn't make it to heaven. Maybe this is hell."

"You don't get to go to hell with a beautiful girl," he replied, putting his arm around me. "Face it, we're alive, and you're stuck with me. Think you can make it back if I help you?"

I nodded my head, not completely trusting myself to speak. Mark had called me beautiful. Never mind that I was a complete mess, with my hair glopped all in my face, no makeup, and my clothes wet and sticking to me in the most unattractive way possible. Mark still thought I was beautiful.

Thanks, again, God.

"I didn't thank you for trying to protect me from the lightning back there," I told him, my voice cracking with emotion. "You were so incredibly brave, Mark. You might have been killed, but still, you — "

"Let's not talk about that anymore," he cut in firmly. "Nice weather we're having, isn't it?"

It was such an everyday sort of remark that I had to giggle, which I guess was Mark's objective. It was true that it had gone back to being a normal summer day. The sun was out, and the dark clouds were gone. It was as if there'd never been any storm, never any lightning, never any close call with death.

With me still limping, we couldn't walk very fast. Our wet clothes dragging us down wasn't helping much, either. I tried not to hang on to Mark, because I could tell he was really hurting, even if he was trying to hide it.

"Maybe someone will come out to rescue us," I said hopefully.

Mark shrugged. "Maybe."

"Yeah, you're right," I told him. "The rangers are probably too busy on the other end." That was where most of the people went on Assateague, especially the surfers. I shivered, hoping none of them had been caught out there on the waves. That's the most dangerous place to be during a storm. But if I knew that, then they had to know it, too. That was some comfort.

I tried not to think about the other people too much; I definitely didn't say anything more to Mark. I wanted him to know that I wasn't one of those girls who cries at every little thing. I knew I'd been hysterical just a few minutes before, but now that it was all over and I had Mark's arm around me, I was feeling strangely calm.

We hadn't walked too far when we discovered a dead pony. It was lying on its side, and there was a long burn mark running down the length of its body where the hair had been scorched off. A slight odor of burning flesh still clung to the air. It was awful. Just awful.

"Only thirty feet away from where we were," said Mark quietly. "Jesus. It might have been us."

He looked at me as soon as he said it, probably wondering how I was taking it. I was okay, but I did feel bad for that poor pony. It looked so forlorn and so alone, lying so unnaturally in the sand.

But I also felt relieved, and grateful that we were the ones looking down sadly at the pony, rather than the other way around. It was almost a happy feeling. That probably sounds sort of sick, but it's the truth.

"At least it didn't feel anything," said Mark. "I'm sure it was dead before it even knew what hit it."

I thought that was an unfortunate choice of words, if you know what I mean. I squeezed Mark's hand tightly. I wasn't the only one with tears in my eyes. Mark was really affected by the sight of that pony, but I guess he figured he had to hide it.

"You know, in a way, it gave its life for us," I said. "I think that lightning bolt was meant for you and me, and he got it instead."

"Jesus, Norrie, what a thing to say!" Mark spluttered, but he was looking very pale under his tan. "The pony got it because he was taller than anything else out here. Don't turn fatalistic on me, okay?" There was a silent pause. "Norrie, what are you doing?"

I had my camera out and was aiming at the pony. "I'm taking a photograph, of course," I told him calmly. "This is what photojournalism is all about, remember? Realism? You know, we should have taken some shots during the storm. I bet we could have sold them to the paper for some big bucks."

Mark stared at me, his mouth gaping wide open.

Then he sort of sank down into the sand. No, it was more like he plopped down, really. Like his legs couldn't hold him anymore, so down he went.

"Norrie," he said, shaking his head and laughing this weird sort of laugh. "You are my kinda girl."

I stopped shooting and went over to him. He was still shaking his head; his whole body was shaking. I think he was having what they call a delayed reaction. I mean, he'd been strong when he'd had to be strong, when I was sobbing hysterically and generally falling apart. But now that I was basically okay, it was his turn to fall apart. I didn't know what to do, so I kept patting him on the back.

"Uh, Mark, are you okay?"

He nodded, but didn't say anything. It was already getting hot again, but he was shivering. I wished I had some dry clothes to give him.

"Look!" I shouted, pointing down the beach. There was a dune buggy coming toward us. I squinted until I recognized two men in park ranger uniforms. One was driving; the other was standing up, his hands holding onto the frame.

"Over here!" I shouted, waving my arms. "We're over here!"

I glanced over to Mark. "It's the cavalry," I joked. "Late as usual."

Mark didn't laugh with me. He was watching the approaching buggy very intently. I don't know, maybe he couldn't believe it was really them. What a bizarre sight we must have made. Me, in spite of my aching foot, jumping up and down for joy, and Mark just sitting perfectly still in the sand, totally out of it.

The dune buggy stopped. "Hey, are you kids okay?" the standing ranger called.

"We are now!" I told him, reaching for Mark's hand. I pulled him to his feet. He still had that dazed look on his face, and he sort of clung to me.

"Now we know for sure we're not dead," he mumbled.

Twelve

"You might have been killed!" Brenda exclaimed, her face set in the horrified expression of an old lady. But that was Brenda for you, fifteen going on fifty.

She'd come over as soon as my parents had said I could have visitors. There wasn't anything wrong with me; the doctor had checked me out thoroughly. But my parents needed to fuss, so I let them.

"Good God, Norrie, you could be dead right now, both of you!" Brenda was flitting around my room, practically wringing her hands. "You really could have been killed!"

"Gee, sorry to disappoint you," I joked from my bed. "Come to think of it, I guess that would have made the story more dramatic."

Brenda turned to face me, her eyes shining with

tears. "It's not funny, Norrie. This could be your funeral. You could be dead, and I'd be feeling guilty for the rest of my life for all those mean things I said to you. I'd never even have gotten a chance to tell you how sorry I am."

"Yeah, I'm sorry, too," I said softly. "Honest, I am."

"About my party," she continued. "I was planning to invite you, you know, to make amends. But then Mark said you were doing something else, so I didn't know what to do. But I wished you could have been there. It just wasn't any fun without you. And I know Mark missed you *a lot*. You could tell."

I smiled. Brenda always did have a knack for saying the right thing.

"And to think you might have been killed!" she repeated.

"We might have been," I agreed. "But we weren't. Just knocked out a bit. It all sounds so exciting now, but I was terrified at the time. Mark was, too, but you'd hardly know it. He was just so incredible."

"Tell me everything that happened," she said. "Right from the beginning, and don't leave anything out!"

So I told her the whole story, word for word, without leaving out a single detail. "That is the most romantic story I've ever heard!" she shrieked, clutching her chest. "I could die! I could just die!" And then she fell back on the bed, making fainting noises like she really was dying. Brenda really is an excellent best friend. No wonder I'd missed her so much.

She sighed. "Isn't this turning out to be the best, most fabulous summer ever? Me and Peter and you and Mark?" She twisted over and looked at me. "You finally managed it! But, really, Norrie, I think you might have found an easier way."

For a second I wasn't sure whether she was kidding me or not.

Smiling, she nudged me. "Don't you remember me once telling you that maybe if Mark got hit by lightning, he'd wake up and realize you were the one for him? I never dreamed you'd take me seriously!"

"Ohmigod, that's right!" I started giggling with her. "Is that Twilight Zone or what?"

We started humming *The Twilight Zone* theme together. "Maybe I'm psychic!" said Brenda.

"More like *Psycho*," I replied, laughing as she threw a pillow at me. Then we got really silly, just like in the old days. We were acting so seventh-gradish that my mother finally had to come in and send Brenda home, saying I needed my rest. I didn't, but Mom was really into her mothering mode, so I let it pass.

"Call you later, Norrie," Brenda said on her way out.

"I'll be here," I replied, reaching for the double-chocolate milk shake Mom had brought up for me. Being mothered has definite advantages.

I used to hate the month of August. First, because it's just too darn hot. Second, because you're starting to get bored with summer, almost ready to go back to school, but only for a few weeks, tops. No way are you looking forward to a whole long, boring year of classes and homework and studying and getting up when it's still dark out.

So naturally in August you begin to feel like you

should be enjoying your last weeks of freedom to the *max*. But can a condemned prisoner really enjoy his last meal, knowing it's his last meal? I mean, the pressure to pack as much as possible into those last weeks is just too much.

But, suddenly, August had become my favorite month. I was alive, and there's nothing like a brush with death to make you appreciate life. I had my best friend back. I was getting along with my parents. I had a great job. And I had Mark. Nothing else seemed to matter very much.

I swear, everything was working out so incredibly well that it kind of worried me.

Suddenly I felt something tickle the end of my nose. "Hey," Mark said softly, "did you fall asleep on me?"

I lazily opened my eyes and looked up at him. We were sitting under a huge tree, and the leaves and sunlight made a dancing lace pattern on his face. I thought he was going to do the Prince Charming routine and kiss me, but he nudged me instead.

"I'm just relaxing," I told him. "That's why we're here, in case you don't remember. This is supposed to be our break from work and from the beach."

We'd driven over to Blackwater Bird Refuge for the day, to have a picnic, do some cycling, and, of course, to take photos of the birds. Blackwater is famous for its wild geese, which pass through in the fall, and for its bald eagles. So far, all we'd seen were a few ducks. Big deal. But it was a great day, even without the birds.

I watched Mark start to pack up his bike with our picnic stuff. Sighing, I lay back and put my hands underneath my head, enjoying the coolness of the shade after cycling in the hot sun. "This sure is different from Assateague, isn't it?"

"Don't," he said, with a shudder, "even mention that place to me."

"Come on, Mark, relax," I told him, following his worried gaze up to the sky. "Lightning doesn't strike twice, you know. Besides which it's an absolutely gorgeous day. Not a cloud in sight."

"Knock on wood," Mark muttered, knocking on the tree twice before sitting down next to me. "I wouldn't want to go through that experience again."

"Oh, I don't know," I said, not thinking of the near-death experience, but of how wonderful Mark had been. "It wasn't *all* bad."

Mark's eyebrows shot up. "Are you high on something? It was — "

I turned my head and smiled. His look of amazement vanished, and then he was smiling, too. "No, it wasn't *all* bad," he agreed huskily. "At least it got us together. We've got something special going here, right?"

I nodded, getting that warm and oozy feeling all over my body again. It was all so tender and romantic that I didn't think I could speak. It wasn't the time for words, anyway. I lifted my head a little, and then Mark was kissing me. Kissing me, touching me, making me feel so good that it almost hurt. On and on it went until I just didn't think I could take it anymore, that I might explode from feeling so good.

"God, Norrie — " Mark whispered shakily against my neck, and I knew that I was doing the same to him.

Just then a group of kids on bikes rode by, their hoots of laughter making us sit up but fast. I fumbled with the button of my shirt, my cheeks burning red in a way that had nothing to do with the sun or cycling.

I glanced nervously over at Mark.

"Aaarrgh," he groaned and fell back to the ground like he'd been shot. He landed with a soft thud, his hand over his heart. I just had to laugh.

"Very funny," he muttered, with a big, dramatic sigh. "Sadist."

I laughed again. We were back to acting normal, but inside I was still feeling extremely un-normal. I mean, of course, I was glad I had this effect on Mark, but it was kind of scary. When he'd been kissing me, I'd felt so *overpowered* — like suddenly I understood how sometimes people can lose control, you know, get caught up in the moment, when before, I'd just thought that was a bunch of bull. I wondered if Mark felt scared, too, but I didn't know how to ask.

He was still lying on the ground, his hands folded across his chest. "I guess we'd better get going," he said, peering at me through one eye.

"Maybe we'd better," I agreed and gave him my hand to help him up. He smiled as he picked some grass out of my hair, but he didn't kiss me again.

We bicycled down the road some more, until we came on a place where lots of cars and people were taking pictures. We didn't understand what all the commotion was about until we got closer.

"*All right*," said Mark, whistling under his breath, and the both of us quickly got our cameras out.

Out in the marsh, perched on a long pole, there was a bald eagle. It was a perfect shot; the day was sunny, with no haze, there were no other trees around, or anything else to get in the way. There was just this beautiful, proud eagle, glaring at all its admirers while the admirers busily clicked away.

"You know, this is the first time I've ever seen an eagle," I whispered to Mark.

"Make the most of it," he advised. "A shot like this doesn't happen too often."

We must have taken about fifty pictures of that eagle, but it never moved. I was beginning to wish it would, just so I could get a shot of it flying off. Only I didn't want to spoil the perfection of that moment, or ruin the shot for somebody else.

Finally, the same group of kids who'd hooted at us before rode up, clapping their hands and making so much noise that the eagle suddenly took off. A great flurry of feathers and he was gone. I dropped to the ground and snapped off ten or twelve frames.

God, I was getting as bad as Mark.

The eagle soared around us once — I was hoping it would swoop down on one of those obnoxious boys, but it didn't — and flew away. The crowd gave a sort of collective moan, watching it until it was well out of sight, like none of us wanted to let it go.

"I'm glad those kids got it to fly," I confessed. "I didn't have the heart to do it myself."

"Me, neither," said Mark, this time helping me up. "I wanted it to fly off, but then come back. That was something everybody should have a chance to see."

That was just what I'd been thinking. Great minds and all that. We held hands while we walked back to our bikes.

Later we climbed the observation tower to use up the rest of our film. The reeds shone like golden wheat growing in a field of blue water, but I knew this picture wouldn't be as perfect as the one I had taken of the eagle flying away. I let Mark use up my roll, too. He was much more into landscape than I was, anyway.

"Should I come over on Sunday after work and help you develop these?" I asked him when he was finished. That was getting to be our usual routine, so I was surprised when Mark shook his head no.

"I've got to go to my brother's with my folks tomorrow. It's a family thing," he explained. "I'm not sure what time we'll get back, but I'll call you, okay?"

"Sure. No problem."

"I would've invited you, but I need one of us here. Sunday is our — "

" — busiest day," I completed for him, without thinking. He looked surprised, and I started to blush. I guess we were both reminded of the time I'd asked for Sunday off to be with my grandmother. Only he still thought I'd been with Brad.

"How much older is your brother?" I asked quickly.

"Five years. But if you met him you'd think he was twenty years older, at least. He's like some middle-aged guy in a Springsteen song, you know what I mean? One kid, another on the way, a house with a big mortgage that he's humping to pay off in some dead-end job. He opted out of college to get married. My parents tried to talk him out of it, but he wouldn't listen."

"I guess people have to live their own lives."

"You call that living? Man, when I think of all the plans he used to have! Some of them made mine look tame." He shook his head. "It just goes to show how love can really screw things up."

"Well, sometimes," I conceded. "But it doesn't have

to be that way. Not with" — I took a deep breath — "not with the right person."

He turned toward me, the breeze ruffling the tendrils around his ears. "Yeah, you might have something there," he said, taking my hand. It had grown very quiet; we stood there silently while several minutes ticked by, watching a heron fly low over the water. This time Mark didn't reach for his camera. Neither did I. We just keep looking at the view, but I, for one, was not really seeing it. I was too distracted by Mark's thumb gently stroking my fingers and knuckles. Back and forth he'd go, then in a circular motion, and then back and forth again. It was such a simple, nothing little thing, and probably Mark didn't even realize he was doing it, but it was sure turning me into goo.

"I really like you, Norrie," Mark said suddenly, and I was so shocked that for a minute, I wasn't sure I'd heard him right. But he was looking at me with that intense way he has, that look that literally curls my toes. Only this time it even more intense; it was like Mark's eyes were laser beams that were melting my insides in the nicest way possible.

The part of me that wasn't melting was singing the Hallelujah Chorus; there was a band playing, and millions of fireworks going off all at once. But all I managed to get out was, "Me, too," in a very shy and un-Norrie like voice. Not much, I know. I didn't want to ruin his concentration just as things were getting good.

"I feel really comfortable around you," he added. "I hope . . . I mean, can I ask you something?"

Uh-oh, I thought. The moment of truth had arrived.

"No, no," Mark exclaimed, catching my look. "I

144

didn't mean *that*. I know we have a ways to go before we get into one of *those* discussions."

"Oh." Considering how much I loved Mark — seriously, I would have laid down and *died* for him at that moment — I was surprised how relieved I felt to hear him say that. I guess I wasn't ready to get into *that* yet. Then I started wondering exactly how long "a ways" was. A month? A year? A *week*?

"I was just going to ask you if you ever think about, you know, that married guy."

Oh, God, not again. Who would have thought that somebody as terrific as Mark could be so insecure?

I shook my head firmly. "No. Never."

"Come on, you couldn't have forgotten about him completely. An older guy like that."

"You're older than me, too."

"Only two years. It doesn't seem like so much anymore."

"Well, maybe I prefer someone closer to my own age."

Mark took a moment to digest that. Then, "He was tall. Good-looking. Sort of like a young Robert Redford."

"Maybe," I said, giving him the once-over, "I prefer dark hair. And dimples. Sort of like a young Tom Cruise."

"Norrie, the guy drives a red Alfa-Romeo."

"Maybe I prefer American cars. Especially if they're very old and beat-up. I'm very patriotic that way."

"Okay, already, I give." He gave me that narrowed-eyed look of his. "You're too much, you know that?"

"Thanks," I said sweetly. "That's the nicest thing you've ever said to me."

He grinned and shook his head at me. "Well at least you know *I'm* not married."

"You'd better not be," I growled. "Or you'll be walking funny for the rest of your life."

I stole that line from somewhere, but it still earned me a laugh. But only a short one.

"I guess honesty is important to you after that experience, huh?" he asked, serious again. "Listen, I feel the same way. That's what burnt me up about that guy the most. Lying to you, lying to his wife. I wonder how often he gets away with it?"

I shrugged. What I wondered was how I could change the subject.

"Man, I hate it when girls lie," he said vehemently. "It's the one thing I just can't tolerate. They tell you one thing, and then you find out it's something else, and what for? Why not just be truthful about whatever it is in the first place? Too many girls like to play games with your head — like dating is some big power struggle, you know what I mean?"

"Uh — I think so."

"But you're too honest for that crap," he added. "That's what I like about you, Norrie."

And that's when my heart stopped.

"I didn't see it at first; I wasn't so sure," Mark continued, totally unaware that I was having a heart attack. "It's just that back at school, I really didn't notice you so much, and when I did, I thought — " He shook his head. "Well, that's not important now. Then, what happened with that married creep made me start to think. But on Assateague — Jesus, you were so brave and . . . tough! Right there and then I knew you couldn't be the type to be anything but completely

146

honest. You have too much guts to do it any other way."

His other hand came up to touch my cheek. He was still looking at me, tenderly, expectantly — I was supposed to say something. He was waiting for me to speak.

You should tell him the truth about Brad, I told myself. There will never be a better time. Get it off your chest, out in the open! Do it, Norrie, do it! Tell him *now*!

I laughed uneasily. "You make me sound like a Marine."

To my own ears I sounded false and guilty as hell; there might as well have been a huge L on my chest for LIAR. But Mark didn't seem to notice.

"As long as you don't look like one," he replied, grinning. "That's the other thing I like about you."

And then he started kissing me again. Long and passionately, like we were two characters from the cover of a romance novel, up there all alone on top of a tower, the golden marsh gently cheering us while we vowed our undying love.

It was so incredibly romantic, and normally I would have keeled over from so much joy. But this time I just couldn't get into it. It was like this claw of terror had gripped my heart and was keeping me from enjoying what should have been the happiest moment of my life.

Mark stopped kissing me when we heard the voices of the kids as they started climbing the stairs. It was the same group that had interrupted us before, the obnoxious brats who had scared the eagle off; this time I was almost glad to see them.

"Jesus, not those monsters again," Mark groaned. "Did your parents hire them to chaperone us?" he demanded. "What, they wanted to make sure we didn't have too much fun?"

I smiled back at him. "If anyone hired them, it was probably one of your old girlfriends," I said, and I knew then that the moment for telling Mark the truth about Brad had passed.

When I got home that night I had an absolutely splitting headache, the worst I've ever had. All the way back to Ocean City, Mark had been so incredibly sweet and loving, until I thought I was going to scream. I felt so *guilty*.

Then — talk about a trip to loony-toony land — this old song came on the radio, the one that goes, "Liar, liar, pants on fire; your nose is longer than a telephone wire." I came very near to blurting out the truth then; I mean, it had to have been a sign from God, right? But I didn't tell him. I couldn't. I just sat there and listened while Mark sang along in his slightly off-key voice. "Liar, liar, pants on fire . . ."

It was awful. By the time we said good night, there were thousands of tiny men in my head pounding away with sledgehammers and they were showing me no mercy. But, then, I don't suppose I deserved any.

I was in the kitchen, getting a glass of water for my aspirin, when the phone rang. I picked up the receiver and then nearly dropped it again. It was like another sign from God.

"Norrie, let me talk to Steffie," said Brad, sounding very serious. He didn't even bother to say hello first, and I hadn't even spoken to him since he got back to Washington from Turkey. Very unlike Brad, who is always so polite and not the type to worry about the cost of long-distance calls.

"Steffie's not here, Brad. What's wrong?"

"Are you sure she's not there?"

"Pretty sure," I told him. "I just came home a little while ago, but the whole place is dark. Want me to go up to my parents' room and ask them? Maybe she was here earlier."

"Your aunt said Steffie told her she was going out with you tonight."

"Oh, well, that explains it," I said. "Aunt Caroline must have gotten me confused with somebody else. I haven't seen that much of Steffie lately."

"I see." There was a second of silence, and then he said, very formally. "I'm sorry for calling so late, Norrie."

"That's okay. I was up. Listen, I'll be talking to her tomorrow" — Boy, was I going to be talking to her tomorrow! — "Do you want me to give her a message?"

"No, no message."

"But you're still coming home next weekend, right?"

"Maybe," he said slowly. "I don't know if I can get away."

"Try to," I urged. "I know Steffie really misses you. We all do."

"You're sweet, Norrie. Take care."

"Bye, Brad — "

But he had hung up already. I guess he'd been just too disappointed to get me instead of Steff. Not that I minded; I was too worried about Mark and me to care about making conversation with him.

I took my aspirin and went upstairs to bed. But I

didn't go to sleep right away. I kept my bedside lamp on and stared at my bulletin board with all my pictures of Mark pasted on it. Mark beamed back at me, honest, truthful Mark, who'd cut down a whole forest of cherry trees before he'd ever tell a lie.

Should I tell him the truth? Would he find out even if I didn't? Wouldn't that be worse? What would he do? How would I tell him?

You have to tell him; you can't tell him; you have to tell him; you can't tell him; it was like a chant pounding in my head.

Sure, I knew I should tell him; honesty is the best policy and all that, but how to do it? Mark hated liars, and I had lied to him about Brad. Of course, I hadn't meant to do it, but would that matter to him? He'd end up hating me, too. Simple logic.

So what was I supposed to do now?

Thirteen

And so I did nothing. I said nothing. I just let it slide, and hoped the worst wouldn't happen. What else could I do? I couldn't talk to Brenda about it — that was still a sore spot between us. I couldn't even get Steffie on the phone to ask her for her advice. She was always out or something, leaving me to face this mess all by myself. The traitor. Of course I did nothing.

I just acted like everything was fine and, strange as it sounds, pretty soon I began believing that everything *was* fine. But, then, acting's always come fairly easy to me. If I weren't going to be a photojournalist, I'd become an actress. A real actress, like Meryl Streep or someone like that, not the kind who makes commercials for feminine hygiene products and zit medicine.

Anyway, I figured I had Mark, and worrying about something that might or might not happen was a waste of energy. I told myself that the only thing I had to worry about was that the most perfect summer of my entire life would soon be coming to an end.

I don't know if this is what they call the power of positive thinking, or if I'd just gone plain mental, but it seemed to work for me. Except that twice I'd woken up suddenly in the middle of the night, my heart pounding, the way you do from a nightmare. Each time I'd tried to remember what it was that had scared me so much, but I never could. It was like the moment I opened my eyes, the dream drifted just out of my reach. But the bad feeling, the feeling of being scared and lonely, stayed behind with me all through the night.

Come morning, of course, I was much too busy and happy to spend time thinking about a bad dream. Busy during the day with work. And happy during the night with Mark. It was still my perfect summer.

"Come on, Bren, hurry it up. The guys will have eaten all the food by the time we get back."

"Just a minute, okay? Let me do something with my hair." She took out her brush and began brushing vigorously. But Brenda's hair is like one of those cardboard ducks in the shooting gallery; it always pops up again. "Oh, God, I *hate* my hair!" she wailed. "Why can't we live in Alaska or someplace where my hair won't frizz?"

"Don't worry about it, the wild look is in. I saw a girl with hair just like yours in *Sassy* last month."

Bren turned away from the mirror, looking a little too wild, *Sassy* or no. "One of these days I'm just going to cut the whole thing off, I really mean it. Start from scratch." She started to fiddle with it again. I stared at my own reflection. My hair could use . . . I don't know what, but *something*. I sighed. Nobody is ever satisfied with their hair.

Mark and I had just spent the last two hours playing miniature golf with Brenda and Peter — their idea of a really hot time. Now Brenda and I were holed up in the bathroom at this Mexican restaurant called Plata Grande. Peter wanted to come here because he's crazy about their guacamole. He's a guacamole fiend, which was probably a good thing, since guacamole was about all we could afford at a nice restaurant like Plata Grande.

The owners of the restaurant had continued the Mexican theme in the bathroom: painted tiles from ceiling to floor, and Spanish music piped in. There were also mirrors everywhere, three-way mirrors that wouldn't let you get away with anything. "I don't know what you're complaining about," I said. "All this exercise I've been getting, and my butt is still big enough to show home movies on."

"Your butt? What about my thighs? They're like cottage cheese! Not to mention my flabby upper arms." She jiggled them to demonstrate. "I've got upper arms like my grandmother, and I'm only fifteen!"

This is sort of an ongoing contest between Brenda and me — who hates her body the worst. I don't know why we play this game. I guess we like to torture ourselves.

"I'll bet Peter likes your arms," I told her. "And I know he likes to play with your hair."

"Yeah, well, I've seen Mark staring at your butt with this disgusting *leer*." She demonstrated the alleged leer, closing one eye and panting like a dog.

"Oh, gross!" I shoved her, laughing. "He does not!"

"Does too."

"Does not!"

We continued like this all the way back to the table. Then we stopped thinking about how fat our bodies were so that we could dig into the (very fattening) food. Is there something wrong with this picture? Like, maybe, logic?

Anyway, Peter had his guacamole, Brenda had nachos, and Mark and I shared something that looked like the Mexican version of pizza.

"What do you guys think?" asked Peter. "Good choice?"

"*Muy bueno*," said Brenda, showing off her first-year Spanish.

"It sure beats Taco Bell," I said, and held up my fingers, sticky with cheese and sauce. I was about to lick them off when Mark, to my surprise, took my hand and started licking them off himself. God, is that romantic or what?

"*Muy delicioso*," he muttered. He took Spanish, too. His eyes looked deeply into mine, reminding me of the kisses I had to look forward to later on that night. I could feel myself go pink.

Unfortunately, this absolutely outstanding moment was ruined when Peter started making smacking noises and pretending to eat Brenda's hand. Then Brenda started to pretend to eat *his* hand, and they did look pretty funny.

"I'm so stuffed, I can hardly walk," said Brenda, when we were finished. "I feel like a little *puerco*."

"Mexican food always makes you feel like that," said Peter. "In an hour, you'll be hungry again."

"Thanks," she said, punching him lightly in the arm. "Is that a comment on how much I eat?" She turned to us, not waiting for his answer. "We're going over to the boardwalk. You guys want to come along?"

Mark and I looked at each other. You could see we were both thinking the same thing. Sure, it was nice to spend time with Brenda and Peter and all, but now we wanted to be *alone*.

"You guys go ahead," said Mark, putting his arm around me. "I've got my car outside, so I can get us home."

"Work tomorrow," I explained. "You know how Sundays are. We need to get — " and then I caught my breath.

A very attractive couple was standing at the entrance, the woman holding one of those frozen drinks, and the man frowning at something she'd said. Steffie and Brad — ohmigod!

" — An early night," I finished quickly, but not quick enough. Mark had seen them, too. His arm on my shoulder tightened, and he moved closer to me, like he was trying to shield me. I tried to look as invisible as possible.

"What's *he* doing here?" he asked. My question exactly. I had thought Brad was still safely in Washington.

"Man, I'd like to pop that jerk one," Mark muttered, his lower lip thrusting out like he really meant it. "Come on, Norrie, let's get out of here."

I scrambled gratefully to my feet, but it was too late. Brad's head was turning in the direction of all that hostility coming from Mark. Then Brad's eyes lit on me and he beamed.

"The nerve of that guy!" Mark hissed. "He's coming over here!"

And he was, dragging Steffie behind him. I just stood there, frozen to the spot. My worst nightmare was about to happen, and there was only one way to stop it.

"Mark, there's something I've been meaning to tell you," I began hurriedly. "It's about Brad and me. You see, he's my cousin's husband."

"What?" Mark's head swung from the rapidly approaching Brad and Steffie back to me. "With your *cousin's* husband?"

"Oh, no, that's just it," I said, but how to explain in fifteen seconds or less? Impossible. Brad was already at our table, greeting everyone and heartily punching me on the arm. "Hey, Norrie, how's my favorite tennis partner?"

I winced. I shot Steffie an agonized look, and felt myself die about a thousand times. She had a hand on his arm, like she was trying to lead him away, but he kept babbling on about how he had just gotten back last night from Washington, and how he would tell me all about his trip when he saw me at my folks' house on Monday. Apparently he was coming over for dinner.

This time I really was dying. Please.

"Maybe we'll see you there," he said, looking at Mark. "Uh, it's Mike, right?"

"Mark," he answered tersely. Okay, now I was dead. Absolutely.

"Right, the boss," said Brad, innocently unaware that he was adding yet another shovelful of dirt on my grave. "So how's the food here? Any good?"

"Excellent," Peter assured him. "Try the guacamole."

"Okay. We will."

"Come on, Brad, I'm hungry," Steffie said, pulling on his arm. He frowned, like he was annoyed with her.

"All right, already. See you kids later."

Then they left. *Finally.* A hostess dressed like a Mexican peasant came and seated them at a table clear across the room. They opened the gargantuan menus that completely covered their faces and started reading them. It still felt like they were next to us.

I glanced nervously at Mark, who looked like he'd just taken a fly ball in the face. An angry red color was creeping up his neck. He stared at me, stunned. Then he turned away and started walking out.

"Mark!" I croaked, finding my voice. "Please wait!"

He kept moving. I ran after him. He stopped once we were outside, turning to me with narrowed, contemptuous eyes.

"You never went out with that guy, did you," he said, more like a statement of fact than a question.

"Well, that was what I was trying to explain to you — "

"And he was never interested in you."

"Not in the way you thought," I admitted. "You see, you misunderstood, and I — "

"And you what? Let me? You used him. Just like you used me."

"No, it wasn't like that, Mark. Please — "

"You lied."

I cringed. "I never actually lied — "

"Oh, *sure* you didn't!"

"I was going to tell you," I insisted desperately, "really I was — "

"Oh, yeah? And when was that going to be?"

I faltered. "If you'll let me explain the whole story, I know you'll understand — "

"Get out of my way."

"But, Mark — "

"I said, get out of my way," he repeated, stepping around me. "Brenda and Peter will take you home. Or you can get a ride home with *your relatives,*" he snarled. "I'm outa here."

I watched him get into his car, feeling fear like a sickness in my stomach. The Mexican pizza wasn't sitting too well; I thought for a moment that I was going to have to run into the bathroom and up-chuck all over their beautiful tiles. But the feeling passed. I wiped my hand over my eyes and went back inside.

Brenda and Peter were waiting for me by the entrance. They looked at me, then at each other, like they weren't sure what they should do and wished like hell they were someplace else.

"Don't worry," Brenda said consolingly. "It'll work out."

"But he was so angry," I cried. "He looked at me like he *hates* me."

158

"Oh, no, he was just mad, that's all. He'll get over it."

"Do you really think so, Bren?"

"Of course," she said loyally. But she didn't sound so sure. Neither was I.

"Gee, it's getting kind of late. Why don't we take you home?" Brenda suggested, nudging Peter.

"Uh — sure thing," he said, "I guess none of us feels like going to the boardwalk now. Work tomorrow, right?"

Brenda nudged him again. She must have been thinking the same thing I was; that one of us — namely, me — might not have a job tomorrow.

Of course, Mark hadn't mentioned anything about firing me, so I'd still have to show up tomorrow. Then maybe I'd get another chance to explain everything to him.

Nobody said much during the short ride home. I could see Brenda looking worriedly at me through the rearview mirror, and then exchanging looks with Peter.

"Want me to come inside?" Brenda asked when we got to my house. "We could talk some more."

I shook my head. "No, I'm all right."

"Okay, but call me later. I don't care how late it is," she said, twisting around in the seat to give me a reassuring smile. "And don't worry about it. Tomorrow you'll be back together again. I'm sure of it."

She didn't really sound any more sure than she had before, but somehow I began to feel more optimistic. Of course, it would all work out. I just had to make sure that it did.

● ● ●

The next morning I washed my face in ice water, trying to get rid of the tear marks. Then I dressed especially carefully in my skimpiest shorts and a neon pink bikini top. I crimped my hair and put it into a side ponytail. I even put on eyeliner.

I wasn't expecting Mark at our usual meeting place and, sure enough, he wasn't there. I hunted around and finally found him down on the boardwalk. He was sitting on a bench, reloading his camera.

"Hi, Mark."

He looked up, the surprise on his face turning to a scowl. He started fiddling with his camera again, ignoring me.

"Can I sit down?"

He shrugged. I tentatively sat down on the far side of the bench. He immediately stood up to leave.

"Come on, Mark, give me a chance to explain, will you?" I pleaded. "Can't you at least spare me five minutes?"

He glared at me, and then at his watch. "Go ahead, I'm counting," he said. "But it's not going to change anything. I'm not a complete bozo, you know."

"I never, ever said you were! You're the smartest guy I know! If you'd only let me explain — "

" — I'm still counting. You've got three and a half minutes left. Go ahead."

I took a deep breath. "Okay. It's true I let you think Brad was more than a friend — "

"Jesus, that's rich. You let me think you were in love with the guy! You let me go on and on, acting like you were really broken up about it, and I believed

160

you! I actually felt sorry for you! That's the only reason I took you out in the first place!"

"Aha!" I pounced. "So now you know why I did it. I had to get your attention. It worked, didn't it?"

"Oh, I get it. It's okay what you did, because you got what you wanted. Jesus, setting us both up that way; that is sleazy — and I used to think you were so innocent!"

That hurt, but I went on. "You were the one who assumed that Brad was my boyfriend. I didn't set either of you up. I just, you know, went along with it. I didn't think it would matter so much, and you were . . . finally paying attention to me. But then you came and told me about Brad being married, and you were so concerned — "

"You must have had a good laugh about that one."

"I never laughed! It was just something that got out of hand. I must have told you a hundred times — a million times — that it had been no big thing, but you wouldn't listen! You wanted to believe this tragic love story that *you* invented, not me! What else was I supposed to do?"

"How about telling the truth? You ever try that?"

I cringed. "By then it was too late, and I didn't know how to."

"You don't know how to tell the truth? Yeah, I guess I can believe that."

"I mean, I couldn't find the right time or place — oh, never mind," I muttered. "What does it matter? What difference does it make now?"

"It makes a hell of a difference to me!"

"Why?"

"It just does, that's all," he replied stonily, crossing his arms over his chest.

I sighed. Oh, why doesn't anything go the way I plan it? By now we should be making up and, instead, Mark was looking madder than before, and I was pretty much fed up myself.

"Okay, you want the truth?" I asked shrilly. "The truth is, you shouldn't be angry. You should be flattered."

"Flattered?"

"That's right, *flattered*! I worked my ass off all year trying to get you to notice me! I took up photography because of you! I joined stupid Yearbook because of you! I even stayed home from the Spring Fling because of you! Okay, so I wasn't so truthful about Brad. He doesn't mind, Steffie doesn't mind, why should you?"

I was panting by the time I finished this speech. But the expression on Mark's face told me I was wasting my breath.

"You just don't get it, do you?" he asked, shaking his head. "Okay, I'm *flattered* that you were interested in me, sure, but that doesn't mean I like being set up — "

"I told you, I didn't set — "

"Okay, then, I don't like being used. *And* I don't like being lied to and made a fool of, either."

"Well, excuse me, when did you become Saint Mark? Tell me, how many different girls have you gone through this summer already?"

That one was a direct hit. But he was back a second later. "I didn't lie to a single one of those girls," he retorted. "And I didn't play games with them, either. That's what this is to you — some little-kid game.

Even on Assateague — Jesus, we almost got killed! — and that was just another part of the freakin' game plan to you."

"That's not true!" I protested, but he ignored me.

"It's like you're on maneuvers — he makes this move, now I make that move, and all that matters is that you win in the end. Coming here today, that's just another move. You put on some clothes you're practically falling out of, and then you cry a little bit. Then I'm supposed to say everything's okay. But, guess what, Norrie? I'm not making that move. The game is over."

"Mark, you've twisted it up all wrong," I said, my heart beating painfully and clearly against the wall of my chest. "I really l-" — I stopped myself in time. But he'd said he wanted honesty, didn't he? — "I love you," I completed, the words wobbling as I forced them out of my mouth. "I love you, and you just don't know how sorry I am about everything. I never meant it to go this far and, I swear, I'll never lie to you again. I'll never lie *period*. But, please, don't be mad anymore. Can't we just forget it?"

He shook his head. "No," he said shortly. "I can't. I'm not mad, Norrie. . . . Okay, maybe I am mad. That'll pass. But I don't think I want to go out with you anymore." He looked away from me. "I'm sorry."

I blinked. "But, Mark, you can't mean — " I reached out to touch him, but he backed off, like he thought I might be contaminated. Stunned, I watched him stand up and put his camera around his neck. He looked grim and very anxious to get away.

"What about my job?" I asked in a small voice.

He shrugged. "You can keep it. Or I can handle the

work myself. I don't care. Summer's almost over, anyway. We'll go back to the way things were at the beginning. Strictly business, all right?"

No, it isn't all right, I wanted to tell him, but I didn't get the chance. He walked off, toward the water and into the sunlight. He left me sitting alone on the beach, with eyeliner running down my cheeks.

Fourteen

"Norrie, what on earth happened to you?" my mother exclaimed when I slammed into the house. Damn. I thought they'd be out somewhere already. Didn't they have a life of their own?

"Why are you crying?" she asked, putting her hands on my shoulders and turning me to face her. "Has something happened, honey?"

"No, nothing," I said, pulling away from her. "I'm okay."

"Norrie!" my father screamed from the kitchen. "Look what I found in the garage, thrown away, rusted through — why can't you take care of anything we give you? Do you know how much these things cost me?" He came in, holding a pair of roller skates from when I was a kid. "You had to have the expensive ones; the ones from Sears wouldn't do. And now I find them hidden in the garage" — He stopped, looking at me for the first time — "*Now* what's the matter?"

"Oh, just leave me alone, both of you!' I sobbed, bolting for the stairs. "Just leave me alone!"

"What did I say?" Dad asked, perplexed. "I just want her to take better care of her things. Is that such a terrible thing to ask? Fine," he shouted behind me. "We'll leave you alone. Our pleasure."

I slammed the door to my room behind me so I wouldn't have to hear him anymore. Then I reached for the phone to call Steffie. It rang seven times before she answered it.

"God, it's early, Norrie," she complained sleepily. "Not everyone gets up at the crack of dawn, you know."

"It's almost lunchtime, Steffie, and this is important," I told her, crying into the receiver. "I don't know what to do. He just b-broke up with me. For good!"

"What? Oh, yes, Mark. Well, take it easy, Norrie. He'll come around eventually."

"No, he meant it," I insisted. "He was cold and mean to me! What did I do that was so wrong?" I wailed. "Why can't he just forget about it?"

"Maybe he just needs more time."

"How much time? And what do I do, meanwhile? Oh, Steffie, if you could have heard him, and seen his face — " I started crying again. "I finally told him I loved him, and he didn't say anything at *all*. It was like he didn't even hear me."

"Norrie, just hang in there, okay? Look, this isn't a good time for me. I can't talk to you now."

"Well, can you call me back?"

"Uh, I don't know. I'll try. But now I've got to go. Brad is waiting for me, and I don't want to get him anymore ticked at me that he already is."

"But, Steff," I protested, "I really need your help. I can't handle this on my own. I swear, I feel like I'm drowning."

"Oh, for Chrissake, Norrie," she exploded suddenly. "So he broke up with you. He'll either come around, or you'll get over him. It's not that big a deal. I've got problems of my own. I'm sorry about last night, but I've got to go."

"Not a big deal! Listen, Steff, you got me into this, now you owe it to me to get me out!" I shouted this last part into a dead receiver. She'd already hung up on me. I slammed the phone down, nearly knocking it off my desk. I felt like throwing it against the wall. How could Steffie turn her back on me like this, just when I needed her the most?

There was a gentle tapping on the door. "Norrie?" my mother asked. "May I come in?"

"What do you want?" I asked between sobs. "I told you, I'm fine!"

"You don't look fine," she said, coming in even though I hadn't really said she could. "What happened to the phone?"

"I needed to talk to Steff and she was *too busy*," I replied viciously. "The phone is fine, I didn't break it, so please don't tell Dad on me."

She ignored that last jibe, sitting down on the bed beside me. "Honey, if I were you, I wouldn't bother with your cousin at the moment," she said quietly. "She has problems of her own."

"That's exactly what she said. What kinds of problems could Steffie possibly have? None as big as mine, I bet."

"Oh, I think you may be wrong about that. Steffie and Brad are having a few difficulties."

I stopped crying. "What kinds of difficulties?" I asked suspiciously.

She sighed. "The usual kind. It isn't easy adjusting to marriage, you know, and being a military wife is especially hard. Brad is away so much of the time. Steffie gets bored and fed up, so that when he is home, they spend too much time arguing."

"Oh, *that*," I said scornfully. "Jeez, Mom, you make it sound so serious, like they might *divorce* or something."

"Frankly, I think they might be headed that way," Mom answered. "Oh, don't look so shocked, honey; you know your cousin wasn't really ready for marriage. She was so excited about getting Brad away from all those other girls, and then having a fancy wedding, that she didn't have time to think about what it would be like to be married to a military man. I don't think she looked much past the wedding ceremony. Probably Brad didn't, either."

"It was a beautiful wedding," I said fervently. "The best."

"Yes, but a wedding only lasts a few hours, honey."

I didn't say anything, but I was thinking very hard. A person needs constants in her life. You know, things that are always true and never change. Like July follows June. Like your parents will always love you. Like Steffie is an expert on guys. Ouch. It hurts to lose one of those constants.

"You must be exaggerating," I said stubbornly. "You'll see, they'll work things out. Absolutely."

"Umm, maybe you're right. Maybe it's just growing pains."

"That's just what I was thinking!"

Mom brushed my bangs back from my forehead and smiled, just like she did when I was a kid. "Norrie, is there something you'd like to tell me? Did you have a fight with Mark?"

She put her arm around me, and I let her. She smelled of suntan lotion and the herbal shampoo she'd used since I was a baby. It was an oddly comforting smell. It made me want to let my head drop to her shoulder and have her hold me while she told me everything was going to be all right. But I was past that age when I believed my mother could fix everything.

"Yes," I admitted, pulling away from her. "But I don't want to talk about it now, Mom. I need to think."

"Okay, honey, I'll be downstairs if you need me." She kissed my cheek and left the room, closing the door behind her.

I opened it again and went into the bathroom. I really meant it when I told her I had some thinking to do. And even at home I like to do my serious thinking in the bathroom. Nobody bothers you in the bathroom. At least my parents don't.

I stared at myself in the bathroom mirror and thought about Steffie and Brad. Of course I didn't know the whole story, but it was true that Steffie had been going out a lot, barely spending any time at all working in Aunt Caroline's shop like she was supposed to. And there was Brad, in Turkey, serving his country. Maybe he'd been lonely. Jealous. That I could understand.

There was a window in the bathroom; it opened to the deck below. I could hear my parents talking about me.

"Did you find out what's the matter?" Dad was asking. "Or is it just the usual teenage tantrum?"

"I'm not sure, but she's terribly upset. Something about a fight with Mark."

"Barbara, you don't think — "

There was a pause, then, "Don't be ridiculous, Bob, she's only fifteen. She'd never do something that foolish, and I don't know how you could even think something like that about your own daughter."

"I'm sure Ellen Hammerskill felt that way, too, and look what happened to Allison. Not much older than Norrie, and she comes in and announces to Ellen that she's going to be a grandmother."

"You don't really believe — " Mom began. I peered out the window and saw the worried look on her face. My own mother! Under other circumstances, it would have been funny. Under these circumstances, it wasn't.

"No, not really," Dad replied, shaking his head. "But these days, you never know — "

"I'll tell you what I know," I said loudly. "I know that if you're going to talk about a person behind her back, you should at least make sure she can't hear every word you say!"

They both looked up at me, their mouths gaping open in surprise. Oh, for a pack of flies to come whizzing by!

170

"Norrie, we didn't mean — "

"*And* for your information," I added, cutting my mother off, "if I were pregnant, I'd be giving birth to a baby named Jesus. I'm crying and upset because Mark just broke up with me. *Satisfied?*"

I slammed the window shut on their guilty-looking faces. They couldn't fool me. I'd seen the relief there before it'd been replaced by sympathy. I could almost hear Dad saying, "Oh, is that all? Thank God." My parents only worried about newsmaking teen problems, like drugs and sex; other more universal problems didn't concern them. Who cared if I was dying of a broken heart, as long as I was still a virgin and wasn't shooting up?

Okay, maybe I was being a little hard on them. They came up later to my room, both of them, and apologized. Dad stood awkwardly in the doorway, like he was afraid to enter in case I might start crying. I actually felt kind of sorry for him. He reached for his wallet and gave me fifty bucks.

"I hate to see you looking so glum," he said heartily. "Go get yourself some pretty new clothes. Take your mother's Visa if that isn't enough. Then when you get home, you can give the old man a fashion show. Is it a deal?"

I looked at the bills in my hand. Dad voluntarily giving me money! Dad offering me the credit card! I must be really bad off!

I stared at him, my face crumpling with tears.

"What'd I say?" he demanded. "I was only trying to help!"

"I know, dear," said Mom, "but a new dress can't solve every problem."

"It couldn't hurt!"

Mom gently pushed him out of the room. "Remember, if you need to talk, we're here for you," she said before she closed the door. "You know we love you, honey."

Well, that was some comfort, I thought, crying into my pillow. At least somebody loves me. Of course, parents don't really have a choice. They have to love their kids, no matter how awful they are. It was one of those constant things.

A best friend is not always a constant, but it should be. These are the times when you really need one. Brenda even broke a date with Peter to commiserate with me. And she called me every day, mentioning Peter only once or twice, and then apologizing when she did.

"Don't be sorry. I'm *glad* you have Peter," I told her bravely a few days after the Plata Grande fiasco. "I don't want you to be unhappy just because I am." I sighed, pushing my sunglasses up on my head and looking out to the sea. "Oh, Bren, do you think I did anything so bad?"

"No, but you know how guys are — they hate feeling like fools. Maybe it's just his pride that's hurt."

"That's exactly what I thought!" I exclaimed excitedly. "And you know he has this thing about honesty. But I just wanted him so much! Why is that so bad?"

"What if he did the same thing to you?" Bren asked. "Would you be mad at him?"

"No, I don't think so," I answered and then, because

I was trying to be as truthful as I could, I said, "maybe . . . oh, who knows? I guess it was wrong. I didn't plan it to get so out of hand. But *he* thinks I was playing some kind of game."

"There are girls like that," said Brenda. "You know, who go in for the thrill of the pursuit."

I thought about my cousin Steffie. "But I'm not like that," I said aloud. "I really loved Mark. I still do."

"I know," Bren said sympathetically. "Oh, it's all just bad timing and even worse luck."

"You can say that again. If I could only get him to talk to me!"

"Have you seen him? Aren't you still working for him?"

I nodded. "But he makes sure we don't run into each other on the beach. I've seen him around, of course." I paused. "To tell you the truth, Bren, I've actually been sort of spying on him. Following him around, making sure he doesn't see me."

"And?"

I sighed. "And nothing. I haven't seen him with any other girls, at least, but he doesn't look all that depressed, either."

I went over to my desk and took out an envelope. "I got this invitation weeks ago," I told Bren. "It's for Mark's opening."

She opened her eyes wide. "You're *going?*"

"If you'll go with me."

"Norrie, I'm not so sure that's a good idea."

"I need to talk to him, Brenda. Maybe he's cooled down by now and is willing to see reason."

"Sure, but this is awfully public. Aren't you afraid?"

"Of what?"

"You know." She gestured helplessly with her hands. "Making a scene."

It figured Brenda would be most afraid of that. I had other things to worry about. "Yes, but I still want to go," I told her. "Come with me, please?"

"Okay," she agreed reluctantly. "You can count me in."

The exhibit was called "Reflections of Ocean City," and it featured two other artists besides Mark. One was a painter, and the other was a woman who did a lot of weird stuff with driftwood. Mark's photographs were the best. This wasn't just my opinion, either; even Brenda agreed with me.

As soon as we walked in, I immediately spotted two pictures of mine: one of the bald eagle at Blackwater Refuge that I'd taken while I was on my back, and the other of the dead pony on Assateague. I was totally blown away, especially by the fact that he had used the one of the dead pony. He'd always said he hated it.

When I looked closer, I saw that Mark had put my name under the photographs. He'd even listed me in the exhibit program as an assistant. My eyes swam with unshed tears. This had to be a good sign.

"Norrie — " Brenda whispered urgently, nudging me. I turned and found Mark standing behind me.

"Hi," he said quietly. "I'm surprised to see you here. I didn't think you'd show up."

"You must have known I would," I countered, somehow managing to sound very cool and adult. "If you didn't want me here, you should have asked for your invitation back."

His lips moved in a grimacelike smile, but even so, the sight of those dimples were enough to melt my backbone.

"You always did have a lot of guts," he said, his eyes glancing around the room. I saw his parents in one corner. They waved at me. I waved back.

"And never the shy type," he muttered. "Come on, I'll get you something to drink."

I shot a look at Brenda, who gave me a thumbs-up signal, and then I followed him into a little kitchen. He poured me a Coke and handed it to me.

"To your opening," I said, raising the little plastic cup. My fingers were trembling slightly, but my voice was firm. "It's good, Mark, really good. So many people! You're a big success!"

"In Ocean City," he amended. "Not exactly the center of the universe. But, thanks."

"Thank *you* for including my pictures," I told him. "I wasn't expecting that."

"You deserved it," he said, pouring himself a drink. "You've improved a lot."

"Due to you." God, were we really having this conversation? It was so phony and unnatural — I felt like I was acting in a soap opera.

"Look," I said, putting down the cup, "this is all wrong. I know you're still angry, and you've got the right, but you have to admit you're getting over it. Putting my photos in your exhibit proves you still care."

"I put them in because they're good. I told you I'd get over being mad."

I smiled and let out the breath I didn't know I'd been holding.

"But this is a good-bye present, Norrie. It doesn't mean I think we should go back to seeing each other. I meant it when I said it was over."

"Don't say that," I pleaded, reaching for his hand. "It doesn't have to be."

"Yes, Norrie," he replied, taking his hand back. "I'm sorry, but it does. I just hope we can still be friends."

Friends? Why didn't he just shoot me and get it over with?

"Don't look at me like that. I said I was sorry," he told me. "Okay, we could have had something, maybe, but I don't like being manipulated, and that's what you did to me. Maybe I'm extra sensitive about stuff like that, but that's just the way I am. I can't change."

"But *I've* changed," I said quickly. "I swear, Mark, if you'd only give me another chance — "

" — Norrie, you are forcing me to say things I don't want to say," he cut in. "I don't want to hurt your feelings."

His voice was as hard and cold as a metal ice-cube tray just out of the freezer. I moved my feet further apart so my knees would stop shaking. "Go ahead," I invited, but it came out more like a dare. "I'm tough enough."

He shook his head, hands on hips, and made a noise of disbelief. "You're too much, you know that? Okay, if that's what you want. . . ." He threw his plastic cup in the garbage can. "The other day, when you said you . . . that you loved me, it got me thinking. I've got a lot to do with my photography and all. Next year I'll be going away to college. Columbia, I hope, in New York. I don't want to get involved in any heavy thing that's going to screw that up."

"You don't really believe I'd screw that up," I said, feeling like I was on the edge of understanding something very important. "Was it because I said I love you? Is that it? Wasn't I supposed to say that?"

He sighed. "Why are you making this so hard for me?"

"Hard for you?" I stared at him in disbelief. Every muscle in my body hurt from the effort not to cry. "This isn't exactly a Disney movie for me, you know. All I'm asking is that you be straight with me. You're the one who values honesty so much."

He turned away from me, his shoulders hunched beneath his blazer. "All right," he burst out. "I don't care for you the way you do for me. I thought I did, but now I'm not so sure. After what happened on Assateague, I sort of got carried away. And, then, finding out that there was no married man, well — that changes things. You aren't even who I thought you were."

"I'm the same girl you were with on Assateague," I replied. "What changed is that you know now that some great-looking older guy isn't after me, so you're suddenly not interested anymore."

"Don't lay this on me, Norrie. You were the one who lied and manipulated — "

" — Yes, I know, I was a real jerk, I admit it. Why don't you admit something, too? Like you're just as big a liar as I am? I let you believe something that wasn't true, but so did you. You said you cared for me, and now you say you don't. You accuse me of playing games. What was it you were doing?"

His eyes narrowed, and his lower lip jutted out, the way it does when he's angry and uncomfortable. "I've been as honest with you as I can be," he said, oh-so-dignified. "I've got to get back to the exhibit."

"Oh, yes, your public is *waiting*," I snapped, and then I let him walk out.

Why is it guys always get to walk out? Why don't we make them stay and take what they've got coming? Why are we always so easy on them?

Brenda was waiting for me outside the kitchen, her eyes troubled and apprehensive. "Oh, Norrie," she said sadly, seeing my tears. "I was afraid this might happen."

"Let's just get the hell out of here, Bren."

Fifteen

So that was how it ended. Finally. Even now, sometimes, the whole thing doesn't seem real. Other times, it seems too real.

I went home that night and wrote the whole story down, from beginning to end. Why, I don't know. Maybe I just like to suffer. Maybe I hoped I'd understand it better once I saw it in black and white. I didn't, not really. But now I've got this story, so maybe I'll read it again sometime when I'm older and wiser. Someday when I'm over Mark. If that day ever comes.

That first week of school was tough, really tough. Like going through hell and having to smile about it. I quit Yearbook. I couldn't bear the thought of being around Mark; it's bad enough seeing him in the hall. Now he's hanging out with this new redheaded girl.

First it was blondes, and now its redheads. No wonder I didn't stand a chance.

He nods his head when he sees me. Once when he was with the redhead, he even smiled. Then came the time he actually said hello. That got me so upset that I cut history and went into my favorite bathroom stall and cried for the entire period. I know that was stupid and pointless, but I couldn't seem to help myself. I was just hurting so *bad*.

It took about a ton of makeup and I still couldn't hide the redness of my eyes. I put on my sunglasses and told my next teacher that I had allergies. Thank God she bought it.

It's three weeks into September now, and we're having our first spell of cool weather. Some places on the boardwalk are already closing down for the season. Today I took my camera — just because I'd quit Yearbook didn't mean I'd given up photography — and went for a walk on the beach.

It was cold and blustery out near the water, but I didn't mind. It was a nice change. The beach was deserted, and that was a nice change, too.

There are these little sandpiper-type birds that run away from the waves when they come in, and then chase after them when they go back out. They're comical to watch, but what's really funny about them is that they'll hop around on one leg. They look like a flock of frantic little peg-leg birds, nervously moving this way and that way, and I knew they'd make a good picture. Only they wouldn't stay still long enough for me to get a shot.

"Come on," I panted, chasing after them. "Relax

for a minute and let me get you in the frame." I aimed my camera, but they hobbled away. I went after them, then stopped, out of breath. How did the little buggers manage to move so fast?

"Bee-u-ti-ful," a cheery voice pronounced a few feet behind me. I turned to find an old man smiling appreciatively. It was embarrassing enough to get caught chasing after and talking to a bunch of birds. What was worse was that next to the old man was a sheepish-looking boy about my own age.

"Young lady, my grandson thinks you're a very pretty girl," he said. "He's too shy to tell you himself."

"*Granddad.*" The boy groaned and turned bright red. He wouldn't even look at me as he started pulling his grandfather away.

"Thanks, but tell him to do his own talking next time," I replied. The old man shrugged his shoulders.

"What can I do? Youth! Wasted on the wrong people!"

I laughed and was surprised to find myself laughing a genuine, honest-to-goodness laugh. Suddenly, just for that moment, I'd felt happy.

So maybe Life isn't over, after all.

I caught the boy's eye as he glanced back at me. I smiled. He smiled back. Where did I get so much nerve? Don't ask me. I'm just glad I haven't lost it.

It looks like I'm going to need it.

About the Author

Laura Sonnenmark was a journalist and a newspaper columnist before turning her hand to writing fiction. *The Lie* is her second novel; her first novel, *Something's Rotten in the State of Maryland,* was an ALA Recommended Book for Reluctant Young Adult Readers and a Junior Library Guild Selection.

Ms. Sonnenmark currently lives in Alexandria, Virginia.

point®

Other books you will enjoy, about real kids like you!

Watch for new titles coming soon!
Available wherever you buy books, or use this order form.